"Brookfield is [...] for the ball. Ju[...] meant for this kind of thing. I don't think it's ever looked more beautiful."

When she looked back into his eyes he smiled again, then looked slowly down over her dress and back up. "Yes, beautiful is the right word."

Rhiannon's breath caught.

She swallowed again. "There's, erm, there's still some food left from the buffet, I think."

She tore her gaze from his, aware that heat was rising on her cheeks as she stepped to one side to show him where the buffet was set up. But, without moving from the same place, he took a hand from his pocket and captured hers, his long, warm fingers immediately tangling with hers.

"Dance with me."

His hand felt wonderful. And yes, she was fully aware that he'd just walked in unannounced, looking the way he did, and she'd pretty much reacted like a shy teenager with a crush. So she turned her head and looked up at him with a challenging quirk of her eyebrows. "How do I even know you can dance? You might have two left feet."

Kane turned round, switching his hands as he leaned a little closer to her face, his deep voice low and deliciously seductive. "Let's find out, shall we?"

Dear Reader,

When my lovely editor mentioned the idea of a Valentine's Day story I jumped at the chance, 'cause what romance author wouldn't love the idea of including the one day of the year when romance is celebrated worldwide? Though, naturally I'm gonna say I think we should all celebrate it every day!

But having two people who had been apart for so long, when they were really meant to be together, finally discover each other again on that special day…well, it called for a little something extra I felt. And what better than a Valentine's Day ball? O-oh how about a Valentine's Day ball set in a gorgeous Irish country manor house? And complete with Austenesque dresses and men in tuxedoes? SIGH…. Bliss to write, I tell you….

So, I hope you enjoy your own Valentine's Day as much as I enjoyed creating *Her One and Only Valentine,* a story of second chances and never giving up on the chance of great love.

And my St. Valentine's Day wish for you is that you may have love in your own life, not just one day of the year, but every day—and always!

H's & K's
Trish

TRISH WYLIE
Her One and Only Valentine

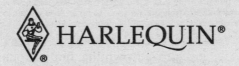

TORONTO • NEW YORK • LONDON
AMSTERDAM • PARIS • SYDNEY • HAMBURG
STOCKHOLM • ATHENS • TOKYO • MILAN • MADRID
PRAGUE • WARSAW • BUDAPEST • AUCKLAND

ISBN-13: 978-0-373-17496-6
ISBN-10: 0-373-17496-9

HER ONE AND ONLY VALENTINE

First North American Publication 2008.

Copyright © 2007 by Trish Wylie.

www.eHarlequin.com

Printed in U.S.A.

Trish Wylie tried various careers before eventually fulfilling her dream of writing. Years spent working in the music industry, in promotions, and teaching little kids about ponies gave her plenty of opportunity to study life and the people around her—which, in Trish's opinion, is a pretty good study course for writing! Living in Ireland, Trish balances her time between writing and horses. If you get to spend your days doing things you love then she thinks that's not doing too badly. You can contact Trish at www.trishwylie.com.

To my readers—the dream makers!

CHAPTER ONE

A TENNIS racquet was the first thing her hand settled on. Anything would have done, to be honest. The fact she had even heard the noise to begin with when it was so stormy outside was miracle enough. But, more than likely, her first night in the huge house alone with her daughter, combined with the thick walls holding the worst of the storm at bay, meant Rhiannon MacNally had more sensitive ears than normal.

And there was *definitely* someone there. She knew for sure as she stepped off the last stair and heard movement, a tremor of fear running up her spine. Going to see who it was probably wasn't the best idea she'd ever had, and she'd always detested heroines in horror movies who went where they were bound to be—well—*eaten*, but this was *her* house now, *damn it*! And she wasn't going to lie cowering in her bed.

So she crept along the hall, ignoring the goose-bumps on her skin and the chill of her bare feet on the slate floor, while her body hugged the wall and she held the tennis racquet in front of her, clasped firmly in both hands.

She froze, her pulse skipping. There it was again. This time a much more distinct rattle, followed by a muffled curse as someone bumped against furniture in the kitchen. So she swallowed hard, ran her tongue over her dry lips and crept closer to the door, fully prepared to scream her lungs out and frighten whoever it was more than they were currently frightening her...

It swung open as she reached out for the handle. And, with a stifled scream in the base of her throat, she raised the racquet to hit whatever might come through.

The shadow moved out towards her, but she sidestepped and swung hard at where she guessed the shadow's waist might be, fully prepared to swing lower than that if the need called, but making enough of a contact to double him up briefly. And she immediately knew it was a *him* from his deep grunt of pain.

He swore in response, moving remarkably fast, catching the end of the racquet, using the fact she didn't let go of it to twist her arm and pushing her much smaller body in tight against the wall so that she was trapped against the cold stone.

'*What the hell—*'

This had been a *big mistake*!

'Get *off* me!' She struggled for all she was worth, desperate to find a way to swing the racquet again. 'I phoned the police; they'll be here any minute! So you better just leave while you can!'

That was a fib, actually; she hadn't been able to find her mobile in the dark but he didn't need to *know* that!

'Rhiannon?'

The sound of her name in such a gruff, rumbling tone stilled her. And then his scent hit her, tingling against her nostrils and attaching to the back of her throat, with low tones of sweet cinnamon and a familiar something else that her memory immediately recognized.

Rhiannon *knew* that scent, even after ten years. She'd never forgotten it, no matter how hard she tried, and now *he* was in her house! He had her *trapped* against a wall! This was a *nightmare*!

'*Kane!*' There was no need to question; she already knew *exactly* who it was. What she didn't get was, 'What the hell are you doing here?'

His warm breath teased the strands of hair touching her forehead, his huge body still pressed along the length of hers. And Rhiannon hated that she was so aware of everywhere he touched, every breath he took, of how his scent opened the door to so many memories.

So she struggled again. 'Get *off* me!'

His large frame remained tight against hers, tension radiating from every pore. 'I'll only consider it if you promise not to hit me with *whatever* that is again.'

'You were lucky I didn't find anything larger or aim any lower, you frightened the life out of me! What in hell are you doing creeping around in the middle of the night? How did you even get in? You shouldn't *be* here! You have no right to just walk in here and—*and*—'

His voice held an amused edge to it. 'Let's cover the frightened part first, shall we? A lone female taking on what I assume she thought was a burglar was a stroke of genius, don't you think? And why *shouldn't* I be here? I've been a guest in this place just as many times as you have over the years. What makes you think I don't still have things here that might belong to me?'

The question flummoxed her for a second, a wave of panic forming in the pit of her stomach, so she took a moment to force it away with several deep breaths. Because he couldn't possibly have meant—

She stopped struggling, sighing a little in resignation when she realized that at least by staying still she didn't feel quite so sensually aware of him. That was a start. Then she took another deep breath and tried to form a coherent line of thought.

'Brookfield is *my house* now. You can't just pop in here when you fancy it now that Mattie is gone! If you have things here that belong to you then you could have got them in daylight, or better still they could have been couriered to you!'

And that way she wouldn't have had to see him or have him within twenty feet of her. 'How *did* you get in? Did you break in? Because if you *did*—'

'I have a key.'

He had a key—since when?

'I'll have that back—*now*.' She scowled up at the dark circle where his face was. 'And could you kindly get the hell off me?'

There was a long pause before he stepped back from her, cold air rushing in to replace the heat of his body. And Rhiannon shivered in response, lifting her empty hand to rub up and down against her arm.

'Now, why are you here, really? Because I sure as hell didn't invite you.'

There was a brief pause. 'We need to talk.'

Rhiannon gaped up at him as she stepped towards the door again. Talking to him in the dark was too disconcerting. 'We have nothing to talk about. And even if we did, which we don't, here's a newsflash for you: there's a new invention called the telephone. You could have tried using one instead of frightening the holy hell out of me in the middle of the night. This is breaking and entering, Mister.'

'Not with a key it's not. And I had a flat tyre or I'd have been here sooner,' his deep voice grumbled behind her as she set the tennis racquet against the wall and felt for the light-switch inside the kitchen door. 'I was reliably informed you wouldn't be here for another week.'

What business was it of his where she was at any given time? She frowned at the switch as she flicked it up and down and nothing happened. She'd assumed she'd blown a light bulb upstairs—apparently not. 'There didn't seem any point in waiting till next week.'

'I tried the lights; your power must be out.'

Great. She sidestepped, bumped her hip off the edge of the dresser and gasped at the pain, automatically flinching back, which brought her up against Kane again, his large hands lifting to grasp her arms.

She *really* needed some light in order to avoid all this accidental physical contact! So that she could look him in the eye and tell him to go *properly*.

His fingers brushed, almost absentmindedly, against the light silky material of her dressing gown, making her all too aware of how she was dressed even before a slight dampness seeped through to the skin on her back from his heavy jacket.

Wind rattled the rain against the kitchen windows as Kane's baritone voice rumbled closer to her ear, an edge of irritation to it. 'Aren't there candles anywhere?'

'*Yes.*' She shrugged her shoulders hard, freeing herself. There had damn well better be candles. Stepping away from him she felt her way along the dresser, hauling open a drawer to blindly search its contents in anger. Of all the things she had managed to unpack during what suddenly felt like the longest day ever, she couldn't recall there being candles or matches, but there had to be some *somewhere*. Had to be!

With Brookfield situated in the middle of nowhere for centuries, it was hardly likely that this was the first power cut it had ever experienced on a stormy New Year's night, right?

She heard Kane moving away, the sound of drawers being rattled open, and for a few minutes they worked in heavy silence, while Rhiannon's fingertips searched frantically until she eventually found what she was looking for. *Yes!*

'I found some.'

There was a rattle from across the large room. 'I've got matches. Stay where you are; I'll come to you.'

With her back against the counter, she waited with bated breath, her skin tingling, eyes wide, while she strained to see him in the darkness. But she didn't have to see; his scent preceded him, so she turned towards him, holding out the candle like a miniature shield.

'Here.'

She'd fully intended him to take it from her, but there was another rattle and the strike of a match that made her blink to adjust her eyes to the bright light as he touched the flame to the candle wick.

Rhiannon's lashes then rose as his face came into focus in the warm glow. He was older, yes, as was she, but he was no less ruggedly handsome than he'd been when she'd known him before. Avoiding him for as long as she had hadn't been an easy thing to do, but somehow she'd managed it, right up until Mattie's funeral.

And she'd had bigger things to deal with then, she hadn't had the time to see what he looked like. Not that she cared any more. But up close and personal, as she was now, she really had no choice but to look…

In the dim light his eyes were so dark they looked black, instead of the deep sapphire blue she remembered. And the fact that he towered over her, his chin dipped a little to study her face while she studied his, meant that she couldn't read any thoughts in those shadowed eyes. Not that she'd probably read much more on a bright summer's day these days. She didn't know him any better now than it had eventually proven she'd known him then.

'Are there more of those?'

The question gave her a reason to turn away, but it was too late to erase the picture of him now seared into her mind. She knew if the candle went out she would still be able to see him— the sheen of short, dark chocolate hair that hugged his head, shorter spikes of it brushing against the top of his forehead from his centre parting—the downward tilt of thick dark brows while he had studied her face—the dense lashes that framed his eyes—the straight line of his nose—the mocking quirk on the corners of his sensual mouth.

Yep, suffice to say, she had a fairly thorough mental image of him. More of one than she would have asked for; *thanks, anyway.*

Holding the candle above the drawer, she searched for more of the same, clearing her throat before she asked in a cool voice, 'Well, what *is* it you want, Kane? Because the sooner I know, the sooner you can leave.'

'I told you, we need to talk. Mattie's death has changed things.'

'*We* have *nothing* to talk about.' But, even as she said the words, she felt an old familiar sliver of fear run up her spine. He'd better not *think* they had anything to talk about! He was ten years too late for that!

'We need to talk about Brookfield.'

They what?

'Why?' Her hand halted halfway out of the drawer with another candle, her face turning to look up at Kane's in the shadows. 'Brookfield is nothing to do with you—Mattie left it *to me.*'

'He left the *house* to you.' His deep voice didn't hold as much as a hint of emotion as he laid the facts on the line for her. 'But I own the estate. And *that means* we need to talk.'

What did he mean—he *owned the estate*? The house and the estate went hand in hand, had done for generations! And, as daunting as the task of taking it on single-handed had been for Rhiannon, she had also been more excited by it than she had by anything else in years. She'd seen it as a challenge she could put her heart and soul into—building not just a home, but a future for herself and Lizzie.

Her gaze shot upwards. *Lizzie!* Rhiannon couldn't have Kane one second more under the same roof as Lizzie!

He read her upward gaze. 'Is she asleep?'

Damn him! She really didn't want to have a discussion about her child with *him.* She wouldn't even deign to answer the simple question when it was *him* asking it. 'What do you mean, you own the estate?'

He shrugged, raindrops on the dark material covering his broad shoulders glistening in the soft candlelight. 'It doesn't take much explaining; I own the estate. Mattie sold it to me a year ago.'

'Why?' She couldn't hold the incredulity from her voice. 'Mattie loved this place; he would never have parted with any of it while he was alive.'

'Under normal circumstances he wouldn't have.' Kane reached out a large hand to turn hers so that he could light the other candle, his dark gaze focused completely on the task, while he continued in a low, almost seductively male tone, 'But he'd overstretched himself on the estate and with all the treatments he tried to get well and he wouldn't accept a loan, so I bought back his shares in Micro-Tech and the estate, on the proviso that I would never sell it separately from the house.'

Oh, this really was a nightmare! Any second now she would wake up—she had to—because this just wasn't happening! And surely he didn't think she could afford to buy it back off him?

'I'm prepared to make you an offer on the house.'

Rhiannon gaped up at him, suddenly aware that his fingers were still curled around hers over the candle. She thrust the other candle at him and the movement dropped hot melted wax on to the back of her hand.

Kane scowled when she gasped. 'We need something to put these candles on.'

'While we have a business meeting in the middle of the night?' She shook her burnt hand to ease the sharp pain on her skin. It focused her mind, gave her a second to calm her thoughts into something resembling sense when all she could really concentrate on was one thing; she had been at Brookfield less than one full day, and already she was in trouble.

And, like all of the main troubles she'd been through in her life, it once again involved Kane damn Healey!

'I hadn't planned on talking to you in the middle of the night. You weren't supposed to be here yet. I've arranged for an estate agent to come value the place tomorrow morning so I had some figures.'

'Behind my back?'

He shrugged. 'If I had figures to show you, then you could make a more informed decision on a price.'

'I've just moved house; I have no intention of moving again.' And she'd given up her job, lifted Lizzie out of school—away from her friends and the only home she'd ever really known. She couldn't do that all over again. The only reason she'd been able to make the decision to uproot them both had been the fact that they would have a home of *their own*.

'You can't support a house this size.'

'You can't tell me what I can and can't do!'

Reaching over her shoulder for a saucer to balance the candle on, his darkened eyes noted how she snatched her shoulder back from him, one hand rising to draw the lapels of her silk dressing gown closer together. And he frowned in annoyance again.

This wasn't going the way he'd planned. Did it ever where Rhiannon MacNally was concerned?

Despite what she may think, he wasn't doing this just to make her life difficult. Because he knew that he was probably the last person she'd want to have dealings with, let alone be forced into any kind of a business partnership with. She'd made it more than plain over the years that she wanted nothing more to do with him.

But he was also pretty sure she couldn't afford to buy the estate off him, so that meant his buying the house made more sense. Then she could do what she wanted with the money. It wouldn't be anything to do with him any more. *Simple*.

Except that already it was more complicated than he'd thought it would be. Being hit in the stomach with what he now knew was a tennis racquet had led to her soft body being pressed against his. And *that* had brought back memories he'd had no intention of ever remembering again.

In the soft candlelight, she was simply stunning.

The intimate arc of light picked up the fine strands of red in her auburn hair, made her doe-brown eyes sparkle when she glanced up at him from beneath long lashes, surrounded her in a halo that made her seem even softer and more feminine than she already looked with her curves barely hidden beneath long, flowing rose-pink silk.

If they'd been two other people, in a different place and different time, then the temptation to be doing something other than talking in the candlelight would almost have been too much to resist.

She'd always been dangerous that way.

Leaning back from her, he dragged his gaze from her face and focused on dropping wax onto the saucer until there was a large enough pool to stand the candle upright while it cooled. Then, as the wind hailed rain against the windows again, he took a breath and glanced at her from beneath hooded eyes.

'It's late. We'll talk about this in the morning.'

Rhiannon's eyes widened. 'You're not *staying* here.'

Oh, for goodness' sake! 'It's a very large house, Rhiannon; you won't even know I'm here till you see me at breakfast.' He smirked. 'I promise not to come looking for you in the dark again.'

The innuendo didn't help. 'I don't want to see you at breakfast. If there's anything else to talk about, then you can come back when Lizzie has gone to school.' She looked away from his face, her gaze flickering upwards again while she frowned. 'Things are already unsettled enough without her asking a dozen questions about *you*.'

It was a feeble excuse, he felt. 'Then I'll wait until she's gone and, after the estate agent comes, we can talk. There isn't a hotel or a B&B for miles.'

'There's nothing to talk *about*!' Her chin rose as she punched the words out and for a moment she almost looked panicked, which didn't make sense to him.

He didn't see what the problem was himself.

'Yes, there is.' With another deep breath to maintain his patience, he leaned his face closer to try and make his point. 'Whether you like it or not, the estate and the house are a partnership and if you won't sell and you don't have the money to buy the land back, then that makes us partners, which means we have some negotiating to do.'

Her large eyes narrowed, her voice icy as she calmly informed him, 'I'd rather chew off my own leg than enter into any kind of a partnership with you.'

He quirked a dark brow. '*Again*, you mean?'

His gaze swept over the flush that immediately rose on her cheeks. Then he tilted his head to the side, his face hovering over hers. 'I thought we made quite a "partnership" last time, didn't you?'

'Oh, you are a complete and utter—'

'Now, that's hardly the right language for the new lady of the manor, is it?'

Her eyes blazed with anger and he smiled. She looked as if she would dearly love to hit him again.

But in a heartbeat she regained her control. Her breasts rose and fell as she took a deep steadying breath and then her lashes lowered before she focused on his chest and informed him through tight lips, 'I don't want to discuss this in the middle of the damn night.' She stepped back and around him. 'So how about you sleep wherever the hell you want? Just make absolutely sure that Lizzie doesn't set eyes on you before you leave. She has no idea who you are and I'd like to keep it that way.'

Kane turned on his heel and stared at her as she pushed the door open, unable to keep the bitterness from his tone. 'Why the hell would it matter to me whether she knows who I am? She's nothing to do with me.'

Rhiannon swore below her breath as she turned in the doorway, her eyes glittering in the candlelight. 'That's the first thing you've said in a *very* long time that I actually agree with. You stay away from her, Kane Healey. I mean it. She'll find out what kind of a low life you are over my dead body.' .

Already irritated that an edge of bitterness had shown in his voice, he scowled at her. What in hell was she talking about?

But, before he could ask, she was gone, the door swinging on its hinges behind her. And he didn't follow, even if it left him clenching his teeth, feeling angrier than he had in a long, long time.

If he'd had any sense at all he would have done any 'talking' through a solicitor. But he had wanted—what?

Frankly, he was already too angry to look for an answer to that. What he *hadn't* wanted was to be made painfully aware of just how much of an effect her presence could have on his libido. And he'd just got that in spades, hadn't he?

The sooner he was out of this place the better.

CHAPTER TWO

'So, Mum, can I get a pony? And maybe a dog?'

Rhiannon smiled affectionately as they made their way out of the cavernous hallway and through the front door to scrunch across the gravel to her Jeep. Lizzie had hidden her first day at school nerves behind incessant chatter all the way through the breakfast that her mother had hurried in order to get them out before Kane appeared from wherever he had slept.

If she'd had her way they'd have eaten slices of toast in the Jeep. Just to be on the safe side.

'How about we get properly settled in first before we stock a zoo?' Though, after the adventure of the night before, a dog might not be a bad idea. They were two females alone in the middle of nowhere, after all. A dog would be a good idea. Something of a manageable size, with a nice deep, scary bark, that could live downstairs in the kitchen.

'Whose car is that?'

Rhiannon's heart sank, her hand on the Jeep's door. She'd so very nearly got away from the house without any questions. *So near and yet so far.*

Pinning a bright smile on her face, she glanced briefly at the sleek, low-slung sports car peeking from the edge of the house. He must have gone into the house at the back.

'It belongs to a friend of Uncle Mattie.' Well, it wasn't a lie. He *had* been a friend of Mattie's, more so the last few years than when she had first met them all.

Lizzie looked all the more intrigued. 'In the house? Why didn't he come down for breakfast? Will I get to meet him after school?'

Not if her Mother had anything to do with it, she wouldn't. 'No, he'll be gone by then. He didn't know we'd moved in yet.' A thought occurred to her. 'How did you know he was a "he"?'

Lizzie shrugged her narrow shoulders, her blue eyes still wide with curiosity. 'Guessed. What's he like? Can't he stay till I meet him? We can talk about Uncle Mattie. I'd like that.'

Rhiannon's heart twisted at the simple statement. Of course she'd want to meet people who'd known her favourite 'uncle'; talking about him was something that Rhiannon had been encouraging her to do. It was healthy. And, much as it killed her to have to deal with it when Lizzie hadn't even reached the grand age of ten yet, she didn't want her to bottle things up. But neither did she want her talking to Kane. *About anything.*

'He's very busy; I'm sure he'll be gone by the time you get back.' The look of disappointment on her daughter's face almost doubled her up with guilt. It was only natural for her to try and reach out for something comforting in the face of so much change. Talking about her Mattie with someone must have seemed an ideal security blanket, 'How about when you come back we go and see what pictures of Uncle Mattie we can find to put on that wall in the library?'

Lizzie brightened a little, her head bobbing up and down, which flicked her long, dark chocolate-brown pony-tail out behind her. 'Okay.'

'Right, well, let's get you to school, then.'

It was only once Lizzie was settled into her new classroom in the primary school, a universe smaller than the city one she was used to, that Rhiannon allowed her thoughts to return to what she had to face back at Brookfield. She wasn't looking forward to it.

And the night before she had tossed and turned, her ears straining to hear any sound of Kane moving around the house, while her thoughts had run riot, trying to cope with how her hatred of him burned like acid in the pit of her stomach as she searched frantically for a quick fix solution to the problem he had presented her with.

Maybe if she'd managed more sleep she might have found an option or two. To have what sleep she had managed uninterrupted by fitful dreams of the past would certainly have helped too…

Tugging angrily on the steering wheel, she made the final turn through the huge wrought iron gates that heralded the entrance to Brookfield.

Having Brookfield and its hundred and something acres to work on was supposed to help both her and Lizzie to focus their intense emotions from Mattie's passing, elsewhere. It was supposed to be a chance to look forwards, not back, and at the same time to allow them to never forget the one person who had helped them when they had needed it most.

They finally had a chance at a real future—the two of them together against the world.

Once through the gates, the Jeep was immediately surrounded by an avenue of tall skeletal trees that wouldn't see leaves for months yet, while Rhiannon thought about the bitterness in Kane's voice when he had asked her why it would matter to him whether or not Lizzie knew who he was.

He had to be out of the house before Lizzie came home; there was no question about *that*!

Even if a small, resentful part of Rhiannon thought for a brief moment that it might do him good to see how amazing and beautiful and bright and funny and audacious her child had turned out to be.

Low branches reached out to scrape against the high roof of the Jeep as she got closer to the one part of her past she had tried hardest to leave behind.

Designed for the coaches that would have driven to the large house when it was first built in the late nineteenth century, the original owners could never have envisaged the need for anything wider than a large coach to use the driveway, so they had simply built it to enter on one side of the lake and leave on the other in one large scenic circle that only ever widened in front of the house itself. It made for a beautiful drive, one that *normally* acted as a soothing balm for Rhiannon's soul.

The trees thinned and allowed a glimpse of the lake and the impressive house beyond. *Brookfield.*

All of her young life, growing up in a block of flats in a poorer part of Dublin, Rhiannon could only have dreamt that a place like Brookfield existed outside a fairy tale. And she still remembered the first weekend Mattie had brought her to his 'little country cottage'. That first turn on to the wide gravel in front of the three-storey country house, when the sun had come out from behind a cloud and glistened in every one of the dozens of small panes of leaded glass, had been like coming home. And it still did that to her, even if the place was now laced with loneliness, without her best friend to greet her at the door. And a rising resentment that Kane Healey was there when Mattie wasn't.

She wouldn't let him take it from her. She'd *find* a way to make it work without the estate.

With a sigh of resignation, she set the handbrake and unclipped her seat belt, but when she walked into the entrance hall there wasn't a sound except the echo of her footsteps on the smooth slate floor. *Nothing.* Not even a whisper.

And yet she could still *sense* Kane's presence.

She moved down the hallway and peeked through doors. Into the lounge, the dining room, the sitting room, the games room and lastly the gigantic kitchen—where she smoothed the palm of her hand over the well worn surface of the gigantic wooden table as she walked to the other end of the room.

Where in hell was he? She shouldn't have to go looking for him!

She raised a hand and kneaded the muscles on the back of her neck where her skin prickled with an awareness of his presence behind her before his deep voice sounded, close enough to make her jump a little, and softer than she remembered it being in a very long time.

'Still tired from the long drive yesterday?'

She lowered her hand. 'Yes.'

'You got your old place all packed up?'

'Yes.'

'And I'll bet you did that on your own too, right?'

'I needed to know where everything was packed so I could find it when it gets here.' She *really* didn't want to make small talk with him.

He nodded as he reached her side, glancing at her briefly from the corner of his eye on the way past. 'That makes sense. Though I'd have thought Stephen might have helped out.'

Rhiannon wasn't about to discuss her disastrous short-lived marriage with him either. So she took a breath and ploughed on in. 'Let's get this out of the way, shall we? I'm not selling you the house.'

'Yes, you mentioned that.' He smiled infuriatingly but, before she could react, he swung a hand towards the large Aga that heated the room. 'Coffee?'

Rhiannon silently groaned, then pinned a sweet smile on her face. 'Oh, please, do make yourself at home.'

'I will. Do you want a cup?'

Not unless he wanted to end up wearing it soon, no. 'I'm fine, thank you. I already *had* breakfast.'

'Yes, with Lizzie. It must be a big day for her, her first day at a new school.'

Even the sound of her name on his lips was enough to twist her gut. Lizzie was her one weakness and Kane had to know that. But having accompanied his words with a narrow-eyed, searching gaze that seemed to see right through her, it proved exactly what she needed to goad her into standing a little taller.

'That would be absolutely none of your business, now, would it?'

Kane blinked slowly, crossing his arms over his broad chest while he considered her. And, just when she was opening her mouth to add something more, he answered in a low drawl, 'You have a real problem with being overly defensive about her; you do know that, right?'

She folded her arms beneath her breasts in a mirror of his stance, frowning back at him. 'And I just wonder why that might be.'

'You tell me.'

Oh, he was a piece of work! In her eyes he was evil personified, even without the additional visual image of being dressed from head to toe in black—black thick-knit polo-neck sweater, black jeans, no doubt black shoes on his large feet. He was the bad guy.

And she'd already spent years honing her hatred.

Unable to look at him for a second more, she unfolded her arms and leaned forward, the palms of her hands flat on the table surface.

'I want you gone. Anything you need to discuss with me about access to *your* land or the use of *my* outbuildings, you can negotiate through a solicitor.'

He smiled a small smile that was far from warm. 'You're overreacting just a tad here, don't you think? There's no need to be immature about this. Just because I hit a nerve when I mentioned your over-protectiveness towards your daughter—'

Her mouth gaped open as he pushed the subject again. Oh, he could *not* be serious, could he? *Immature? Over-protective?*

She pushed her hands against the table, glowering at him as she ground out the words from between her clenched teeth. 'I'm only over-protective when it comes to keeping her away from *you*! And actually, for your information, I learnt to be mature fast. Motherhood will do that to you.'

'Bound to, when you have a baby so young.' He enunciated each word with a calm voice that Rhiannon dearly wanted to slap him for.

She would never have believed she had it in her to hate one person so much!

'Go away, Kane. Go away and don't ever come back. I won't let you hurt Lizzie. You even think for one second about playing daddy to her after all this time—'

He swore viciously, silencing her.

'Why the hell would I want to play daddy?' Unfolding his arms, his large hands bunched into fists at his sides, his blue eyes flaring with the same anger she could hear in his clipped voice. 'She *has* a father.'

'The hell she does! Her father wanted nothing to do with her from before she was even born!'

Kane scowled darkly. 'He married you, didn't he? I'd say that proved he wanted something to do with her.'

Rhiannon's breath caught, her chest cramping, and she even flinched back from him as if he'd slapped her with an invisible hand.

'Is that what you told yourself?' She shook her head in amazement, stunned not only by his words, but by the fact that hearing them still had the power to sting so badly. 'That she was someone else's child? Oh, you're really something, aren't you?'

For the first time, her words seemed to confuse him. 'What the hell are you talking about now?'

A tension-filled silence fell while Kane scowled darkly and Rhiannon shook with years of suppressed anger and resentment. So when the ancient doorbell jangled above the door behind her head she jumped at the sound, her eyes drawn to the small brass bell labelled 'Front'.

Kane was still scowling when she looked back at him. 'That has to be the estate agent.'

'Fine, then you can deal with that on your way out. There's no need for them to look at the house because it's *not for sale*.'

She was halfway across the hall towards the library when Kane blocked her way, his hand reaching out to catch hold of her arm. Long fingers circled and squeezed in silent warning— warning her to stay put because he wasn't done—while the heat of his touch seeped through her skin, radiating into her chilled blood.

'What do you mean, "*someone else's* child"?'

Rhiannon had to tilt her head up to look into his face, hissing the words up at him without trying to hide any of the venom held inside. 'I really don't care what you told yourself to ease your conscience. But the simple fact is you gave up the right to Lizzie a long time ago and popping in on some pretence to see how she's doing now won't fix that. I've made damn sure she has no idea who you really are. So keep your distance. Because if you hurt her, I'll kill you, I *swear* I will. She doesn't need to know what a disappointment her father is.'

The hold on her arm tightened when she tried to jerk free. 'Are you telling me that Lizzie is *mine*?'

Rhiannon swore under her breath as she tried again to tug her arm free. 'Let me go, Kane!'

'*Are you* telling me that she's *my child*?'

She tugged again, her focus drawn to where he was holding

her, while her mind sought frantically for a way she might possibly break free. How dared he use physical strength to subdue her? How dared he make her body burn from that touch when it was meant to do nothing but dominate her?

'Rhiannon!' The tone in his voice changed, with an edge of what could *almost* have sounded like hope to her disbelieving ears.

Which drew her gaze back to his face, and what she saw there shocked her to the core.

'Of course she's yours.' She shook her head in amazement, 'How can you not have known that? When I sent you that letter I made it more than plain—'

'What letter?'

CHAPTER THREE

THE front doorbell rang and rang until Kane had no choice but to release her and deal with it.

Rhiannon stood in the doorway of the library, her back against the wood frame, trying to make sense of what had just happened. He had genuinely looked as if he hadn't known, as if it had been a complete shock to him. He had even looked as if it mattered to him. But that couldn't be right. How could he *not* have known?

And yet the look on his face had been so raw, so unguarded, so—*real*—that it was hard to deny the truth of it. When Rhiannon had always *believed*—

No—had *known*. She shook her head. This had to be some kind of game. Something he'd convinced himself of so he could sleep better at night.

Turning away from the door, she jumped when his voice sounded from the hall behind her.

'Oh, no, you don't. You and I quite obviously need to have a *long* talk.'

When she looked over her shoulder he was walking her way with an expression of dark determination that sent her nerve-endings fluttering again.

'What about the estate agent?'

'I told them to reschedule. It'll wait. *This won't.*'

She didn't want to talk to him any more. It was too surreal, too much to take in or understand, and she was suddenly tired beyond the levels of normal exhaustion.

And it wasn't just a physical exhaustion either. Two of the most stressful things in life were supposed to be moving house and the loss of a loved one—and she'd suffered both in the last couple of months. So, on top of those things, to have to face *this* now… *Well…*

'We'll go into the sitting room. I'm not standing in a hallway while this is straightened out.'

Now he was directing her around her own home? Was there no end to his ability to rub her up the wrong way?

She lifted her chin and marched past his large body, careful not to brush against him on the way. 'We'll go into the stove room; it's more private in there if I'm going to argue with you again.'

Sound was less likely to carry anywhere from the room at the edge of the basement, with the sturdy stone walls that had belonged to the house when it started life as a fortified farm to act as a sound buffer. Lord alone knew there had been double the visitors she'd been expecting in the last twenty-four hours as it was! The last thing she needed was the part-time house-keeper or a visitor from the estate to pop in and hear all of the dirty laundry from her past aired!

But with the large stove in an archway at one side not having been lit for weeks there was a distinct chill in the room—a blessing on a hot day, few and far between as they could be—but not at a time when Rhiannon could have done with some welcoming warmth from *somewhere*.

In front of the empty stove she turned to face him, watching with cautious eyes as he closed the low door behind him before throwing an angry glare at her as he walked towards the high-set window that looked upwards on to the garden. He began to pace, anger radiating from every pore of his large body.

Rhiannon watched and waited, her breath held still in her chest as she contemplated what tactic he would try next, while still aware on a subliminal level of the way he moved—with a kind of harnessed inner strength, a presence that demanded attention without any words…

'Tell me about this supposed letter you sent.'

Her eyes widened. '*Supposed*? That's a joke, right?'

The pacing stopped and he cocked his head at a sarcastic angle. 'Do I *look* like I'm joking?'

Well, no, but… 'You know damn rightly what letter I'm talking about! The issue here, if there *is* one, is why you never had the basic courtesy to answer it—even if it was to tell me not to have her!'

Kane swore so viciously that Rhiannon baulked, even before she had time to be angry with herself for saying what she just had. She'd long since ceased to care why he'd done what he had and there was no way in hell she would let him think it still mattered.

'Is that what you honestly thought I'd do?'

'How did I know *what* you'd do? It was made plainly obvious to me that I didn't know you at all!'

And she'd made it sound as if she cared—*again*!

He looked as if he'd dearly love to hit something but threw another dark scowl at her before he leaned his large hands on the back of the sofa between them. Then he took a deep breath, looking around the room for a moment before he pushed back against his hands and began pacing up and down. And up and down.

One of those same large hands rose to rake long fingers through his thick hair, his head tilting back for a moment as he searched the low vaulted ceiling.

'And where exactly did you send this letter?'

Not that he deserved an answer, but, 'In your locker at the University. I pushed it through the top of the door. So the *it got lost in the post* excuse won't wash. You *had* to clear your locker out.'

She took another breath, shaking her head as her shoulders slumped, a bone-tired weariness settling on them like a dead weight. 'But it's history. Whatever reasons you had for not wanting to know Lizzie don't matter any more. What matters is that she doesn't get hurt in the here and now. That's all I care about.'

Kane stopped pacing, his brow creasing below the wisps of hair brushing against his forehead. Then, just like that, the frown momentarily disappeared, a far-off look in his eyes as his rumbling voice swiftly followed with an edge of realization.

'I had someone clear it out for me when I left. I told them there was nothing in there I needed, that they could keep the books they wanted and dump the rest.'

What was he talking about?

Rhiannon tried to focus her exhausted mind. Then her eyes widened in disbelief. 'You're seriously trying to tell me *now*, after *ten years*, that you *never got it*? Oh, surely you can do better than that?'

He glared again.

'That *is* what you're saying.' Full of incredulity, she repeated the words, as if somehow saying them again would make it real for her. Surely he couldn't be serious? But if he hadn't got it— no, that wasn't right. It couldn't be. She'd always believed—

The letter that she had spent days debating writing; the one that she had carried clenched in her hand while she'd stood in front of the locker, willing herself to put it in. The one he had completely ignored, which had laid the first foundation stones for the resentment and hatred she had carried for more than ten years…and he hadn't got it?

'Didn't it ever occur to you when I didn't reply that I might not have got it?'

She frowned at the question, the chill in the room seeping into her already tired bones, forcing her to shake inwardly. She sat down on the large stuffed chair closest to the wood-burning stove and tangled her cold fingers together on her lap.

Reluctantly she admitted the truth. 'Maybe for a very brief moment, but after the way you just disappeared off the face of the earth—'

'You figured that you'd made enough of an effort and to hell with me?'

'No!' She stared into his angry eyes, not prepared to even contemplate the notion that she might have been at fault during a time when she'd had so many important decisions to make— *alone*. '*You* were the one who had an overnight personality transplant and then left! Do you think that at eighteen, with no well paid career in my near future, that I was ready to face having a baby on my own? Get real.'

'But you still had her.'

She wasn't even going to grace that with a comeback. It had never occurred to her for a single second not to—no matter how terrified she had been at the time. And it wasn't because she'd wanted a part of Kane or to remain tied to him in some way. They hadn't been together long enough for her to form that kind of attachment, had they?

No, from the moment the test had turned blue Lizzie had been *hers*—a part of *her*. And she had done her best to forget where the other part of her beautiful child came from.

'You'd already made it plain that you didn't want to be tied down, by *anyone* or *anything*. When you didn't respond to the letter I assumed you wanted nothing to do with the responsibility of a baby. You can't be *that* surprised that I'd make that assumption. And I wasn't going to chase after you to beg for a handout either. I'd made the choice to have her, so caring for her needs was down to me too.'

It was the condensed version and Rhiannon knew it. But none of her explanation seemed to placate him any. In fact, if anything, he was looking at her with the same incredulity she'd felt only moments before, as if he couldn't possibly understand why she'd done what she had.

'As her father I had certain rights. I still do.'

Her shaking increased. Because she hadn't paid as much attention to the first part of what he'd said. 'What do you mean, you *still do*?'

'If she's my child, Rhiannon, then you've already had nearly ten years alone with her.'

She couldn't—he couldn't just—

When she managed to speak her voice came out smaller than she could ever remember it sounding before. She'd never allowed herself to feel like some helpless waif of a female before. Not once. No matter what life had thrown at her. But he couldn't—

'I won't let you take her from me.'

Because money could buy practically anything as far as some people were concerned, couldn't it? She'd fight with her dying breath to stop him.

Kane swore again. 'What the hell kind of man do you take me for? Of course I'm not bloody well going to take her from her mother! But I have a right to spend time with her, to be a part of her life. And you took that right from me. I can't believe that you thought for one second I *wouldn't* be angry about that!'

Rhiannon wrapped her arms around her body, pressing them in tight as if she could somehow force the inner shaking away while she continued to stare up at him. 'You knew I had a baby. Many things you may have been, but stupid wasn't one of them. Surely you were able to do the maths?'

His jaw clenched. 'You married Stephen.'

Rhiannon's jaw dropped—literally. 'And you assumed that meant that Lizzie was *his*?'

'Apparently I wasn't the only one making assumptions back then.'

Nice try. They might not have been head over heels in love, but he had automatically assumed she'd jumped straight into bed with someone else the second they had split up or, worse still, might even have been with him at the same time. That told her exactly what he thought of her, didn't it? He probably even thought that, coming from the background she had, any rich guy would do!

Rhiannon couldn't bear to be in the same room with him any more. She really couldn't.

Unfolding her arms, she stood up as tall as her five foot eight would allow. 'Well, if you're so certain that's the kind of person I am, then maybe I *am* mistaken about who her father is. I'll have to check through that long list of people I was sleeping with, won't I?'

He had her lower arm caught in yet another tight grip in the blink of an eye as she tried to leave the room. He tugged, just once, but with the shock of his hot hand on her cold skin it was enough to unbalance her and tip her in against his hard body.

Again.

No matter what she did, she seemed to end up being touched by him or trapped close to his body. Where his very male spiced scent invaded her nostrils so that she could almost taste the cinnamon undertones in the back of her throat and where the blazing heat of him immediately filtered through both layers of clothing to burn her chilled body—like being doused in boiling water after lying in ice.

Rhiannon gasped silently, her eyes focused on the column of his neck as she pushed against the wall of his broad chest with her free hand. But he already had his other hand pressed into the small of her back, his arm holding her still.

'I need to know if she's mine.'

Rhiannon swallowed hard while she tried to stay still, to ignore the building heat and the knot in her stomach because it was the way it had always been with them—physical awareness, in its purest form, on its most basic level—instant and powerfully overwhelming. It was exactly this—*chemistry* — that had drawn them together the first time. But she didn't want it to be there this time. She was mature enough now to know that there was more to any relationship worth having than just the physical. Even if the physical had given her the one person in her life she could love without reservation.

Slowly her gaze rose, following a ribbed line of dark wool upwards, over the fold of the polo-neck where it met his deeply tanned skin, over the tense line of his mouth, until she was looking into his blue eyes.

She searched, from one to the other, willing her heartbeat to settle at the sight of the fierce determination there, the need she could see to know the truth. It almost made him look vulnerable. When he was the least vulnerable person she knew.

Whatever it was, it forced the truth from her lips. 'No matter what you think, there wasn't anyone else. There's no question of her not being yours.'

There had never been any question. And, even if there had, the evidence was staring her in the face when she looked at him. It had been the hardest thing about watching Lizzie growing up. Every day she would do something, say something, or simply smile a certain way—and Rhiannon would see Kane in her. And it was only the completely overwhelming love she'd felt from the moment she'd first held her in her arms that had stopped her from hating that those reminders were there.

Kane exhaled, his peppermint-scented breath washing over

her face as the hold on her arm loosened a little, his voice still strained. 'You should have told me.'

'I thought I had.'

'No, because if you had I'd have been there.'

'But you weren't there.' Her gaze lowered to his mouth, to the parting in his lips. 'You'd already gone.'

When he didn't reply she risked another upward glance to discover he was examining the top of her head with heavy-lidded eyes.

Then, just like that, he let go, stepped back a little, his hands shoving deep into the pockets of his dark jeans. 'I'm here now. And I'm not going anywhere until I get to know my child.'

She looked back at his neck and watched it convulse as he swallowed, unable to face up to the fact that a part of her—a minuscule part—ached at the possibility that she may have made a mistake by holding a grudge for so long. Had she let pain and confusion cloud her judgement? As an adult, shouldn't she have been able to see past those things? Had she hidden behind hating him?

No. How had he *not* known?

He tilted his head closer to warn her in dangerous tones, 'And there's not much point in trying to argue about it because I'm not going away this time.'

Rhiannon's heart thudded painfully against her breastbone, her breathing shallow. 'I can't just dump you on her like that—out of nowhere…'

His mouth twisted cruelly. 'Did you *ever* plan on telling *her*?'

'When she was old enough to decide whether or not she wanted to find you, I'd have told her. It would have been her decision.'

'But you wouldn't have encouraged her to ask…'

Maybe not, and it was a moot point now. But Lizzie was bright; already she was asking the odd question about her dad—Father's Day in particular guaranteeing a natural curiosity over the last few years. She'd even made a card for him when she was six. And it had broken Rhiannon's heart, for failing to give her the kind of father she deserved.

'It would have been her decision.'

'She has as much of a right to know as I did.'

He wasn't letting go, was he? Was this what he'd have been like if he'd known all that time ago? Was this the proof she needed to accept that he really hadn't known?

It was, wasn't it? No matter how much she still wanted to believe that he'd known all along, she couldn't deny the possibility that he hadn't any more. It was written all over him. And a very small part of her felt a hole form inside her chest—one that was swiftly beginning to fill with guilt.

Had she maybe known all along that he hadn't known? Had a part of her wanted to keep Lizzie from him? If that was the case, then why had she been so angry with him for so long?

Kane spread his feet a little wider apart as he stood tall to his full six foot two again, towering over her. 'It's like this, Rhiannon—if you don't tell her who I am, then I will. Or we go the legal route. Either way, now that I *do* know she's mine, I plan on being part of her life. And there's nothing you can do to stop that happening. Not this time.'

Even without holding her, with several *safer* inches separating them, Rhiannon knew he had her trapped. Now that he knew and was determined to be a part of Lizzie's life, he wouldn't change his mind, would he? She knew that from the various tales she'd heard over the years—of his determination and single-mindedness in business, his knack of always getting what he wanted in spite of the odds. And, after all, she had been one of those 'things' once, hadn't she?

It wouldn't matter where she ran to if she left Brookfield. Now that he knew…

What she needed was a way of making this work without causing any more damage. 'I need some time.'

'You've *had* ten years.'

'I'll *tell her.*' She glared up at him, making it crystal clear she wasn't happy about it. 'But I'm not going to collect her from school and just announce it. She's just had to adjust to losing her home, her friends at school, an uncle she adored… I can't just land a new father on her too.'

His jaw clenched, his large body even rocked forwards a little. And Rhiannon stood taller, prepared for whatever he would throw her way. But he corrected himself, rocking back as his rumbling voice resonated from deep inside his chest.

'I'll stay here until she's more comfortable with me.'

Rhiannon's eyes widened. 'You can't—'

'Can't I?' He quirked a brow again. 'There are two ways to play this: the easy way and the hard way. You tell me which way you think would be best for her. Because, frankly, right this minute, I don't give a damn what suits you best.'

Her mind swiftly filled in various versions of the 'hard way'. If he chose to fight for Lizzie she would put up one hell of a fight. But was that really what was best for Lizzie?

As if somehow seeing into her mind, he forced the point home for good measure. 'And if it comes down to a legal battle over this then we both know I can afford to fight it for as long as it takes.'

Rhiannon momentarily felt dizzy.

'I'll go and make arrangements to have equipment sent up from Dublin so I can work from here.'

Just like that? He was already making plans to move in?

'And I'll spend time with her when she gets home from school.'

He'd be right here, under the same roof, where she would have to stand by and watch as he tried to bond with Lizzie.

'And then you'll tell her who I am.'

From somewhere she finally found some words. 'You can't be like *this* with her. You'll have to try being *nice*.'

A sudden burst of sharp laughter caught her off guard. A laugh of disbelief, as if he didn't know how she'd just had the audacity to say what she had.

'Ah, but *she* didn't hold this back from me, did she? Why would I be angry at *her*?'

Rhiannon shook her head, a deathly sense of calm washing over her in the face of the inevitable. 'Fine. I obviously don't have a choice. And, to be honest, I'm done arguing with the people living under the same roof as me, even if they're only staying temporarily.'

'What the hell does that mean?'

And that just proved how vulnerable she was in her current state of emotional exhaustion, if 'secrets' were spilling out. 'It means that I have to tell her if you're determined to have access to her, because I won't put her through a battle. But she does need to spend some time with you and settle into her life here first. And that's a request for her sake, not for mine.'

'We're not talking months when it comes to telling her. I'm not even talking weeks. I'm talking days—within the week. Otherwise *I* tell her.'

Rhiannon closed her eyes for a moment. The temptation to run was so strong it was like a fishing line tugging at the back of her sweater. But she'd promised herself when they came to Brookfield that it would be the last time they moved.

When she opened her eyes Kane was studying her, a deep vertical frown line between his blue eyes—a sign that he frowned often, no doubt. But in the depths of his eyes there wasn't just anger, there was something else—a mixture of what looked like consideration of a puzzle yet to be solved, as if he was somehow trying to size her up.

And, for some reason, Rhiannon found herself fascinated by that, distracted even. For a heartbeat she forgot all the difficulties between them and was curious about the man who stood in front of her. Had he really been the person she'd once thought he was or had he lied to her all along? Why had he left the way he had? What had driven him to be so successful when he could simply have sat back and lived on the money his family already had?

Who *was* Kane Healey, *really*?

But all she really wanted to know was whether he could be the kind of father that Lizzie deserved. She prayed he could be. And now he was going to be a part of her life, and Rhiannon knew she was going to have to learn to live with that.

Because the sooner everything was sorted out, the sooner he would go.

She ran the tip of her tongue over her lips and fixed her gaze at a point past Kane's shoulder. 'I'll tell her as soon as she's comfortable with you. But we can't argue in front of her like this. If you have anything to say to me, you say it when she's not here. She shouldn't have to pay the price for our dislike of each other.'

Kane stepped sideways, his upper arm brushing briefly against her shoulder as he walked past, causing a sudden crackle of static to pass through the wool to her skin.

'She's lived her entire life without a father. I'd say she's already paid, wouldn't you?'

Rhiannon stood in the cold room for a long time after he left, her eyes dry and sore, while inside she felt—nothing, as if a part of her had just given up. It occurred to her that she should at least have wanted to cry, just a little, while she was alone.

But, with a resigned sigh, she knew a part of her *had* always known this day would come. All she had to do now was find the right words to explain it to Lizzie.

And a way to live under the same roof as the man she had spent a decade of her life hating.

CHAPTER FOUR

KANE looked out of his office's floor-to-ceiling windows, over the city and the River Liffey far below, swinging back and forth in his chair while he tapped one long finger against his chin.

It was the first time in years that he'd felt so completely floored, thrown by something he really hadn't been prepared for. To suddenly discover that Rhiannon had kept that big a secret from him for so long—

Well, suffice to say it had been a long time since he'd been so angry at anyone; usually he considered himself an even-tempered kind of a guy. After all, he was more aware than most of how life could be too short to get heated up over things.

But how could she have possibly thought he wouldn't have cared that he had a child? Hadn't she known him at all? Did she honestly think he'd have walked away from something like that? Damn her!

'So, basically the offer is on the table.' His corporate solicitor continued talking behind him. 'The shareholders—and you are, of course, a major one—stand to make a fortune.'

He forced his mind to follow the conversation. 'If they vote to accept it.'

'Well, obviously there are still months of negotiations but I'd say it's a safe bet they will.'

Kane continued swinging back and forth, his mind elsewhere. It was a bad time for him to be forced away from the office too… But for the first time in years he had something infinitely more important than his company and his work to think of. *Nothing* was more important than getting to know his child. Not even an attempt from an overseas company to make a takeover. Takeovers he could deal with, shareholders he could deal with, million dollar technological developments he was used to dealing with on an almost weekly basis. The time with his child that he'd had stolen from him was something he would never, *ever* deal with.

How in hell could Rhiannon live with herself? All right, maybe not so much when it came to how he would feel, but to have deprived her daughter of her father…?

'It's a once in a lifetime offer, Kane. How many men are self-made millionaires before they're thirty-two?'

Kane took a breath. 'How many men can stand by and watch something they put their soul into split up into tiny pieces and swallowed by a company seeking worldwide domination of the market?' He swung the chair around to look the older man in the eye. 'It'll mean a loss of creative control and some major job losses. And neither of those things sit well with me.'

Particularly the latter—because the value of family might not mean much to Rhiannon MacNally, but it meant something to Kane. As far as he was concerned, people came first.

'Well, yes.' The man looked vaguely confused at Kane's lack of enthusiasm. 'But this sort of thing happens all the time; it's the way of the world. Job losses happen every day.'

He studied his adviser for long silent minutes. He'd built Micro-Tech from virtually nothing with the help of a small group of investors and, of course, Mattie Blair's faith. But, regardless of what had driven him to succeed, Kane still found it difficult to let go, even for such a large financial reward. Yes, he could agree to it all—to the takeover and the job losses—but he would have a problem looking in the mirror in the mornings. And now that he had a daughter it seemed even more important to him that he was able to do that.

He swung his chair back towards the windows, not allowing his gaze to stray towards the vicinity of Trinity University, where he had first met Rhiannon, while he focused on more important thoughts.

It might not make much sense to want to be the sort of man a child would feel proud to have as a father when that child had lived almost a decade with an *absentee father*, but it was how Kane felt. If she was his then he had to step up and try to make up for the years Rhiannon had stolen from them both.

He frowned at the view in front of him. Maybe he should have figured it out, believed in what they had had at the time so that he hadn't been so quick to think she'd moved on to someone else the second he was gone. But he'd had so much to deal with, had been so eaten up with bitterness and anger and an inevitable sense of fear…

Whereas Rhiannon had thought a letter was enough to ease her damn conscience!

He had to focus on the here and now. What he needed was a plan. Maybe a plan would make him feel better, more in control, more proactive.

Step one was the knowledge that the loss of jobs involved in a takeover would have a devastating effect on a lot of people and their families—people who had gone out on a limb with him in the first place. And he couldn't allow that to happen if he wanted to be the kind of self-respecting father any child deserved.

Step two, as he sung his chair back round again, was to make sure everyone was clear where he stood—and quickly—so that he could get back to Brookfield to right a wrong that he may well have to admit to being part of, because he'd left when he had.

And that meant that part of step three would have to be to discover just how much of a difference his leaving had made to Rhiannon's decision. Because he needed to understand, not so that he could forgive her—he doubted that was even possible—but so he could at least find a way to deal with her.

After all, she was the mother of his child.

'Every kid should have a dog, don't you think, Kane?'

'Not every kid does, though.'

'Yeah, but they *should*.'

Kane smiled patiently at her. 'You don't give up easy, do you?'

Lizzie shrugged. 'Mum says I get my determine…detre…'

'Determination?'

She smiled. 'Yeah, that thing. I always get the word wrong. Anyway, she says I get it from my dad.' She shrugged. 'It's s'posed to be a good thing.'

He nodded in agreement. 'It can be; it helps you get the things you need to get.'

'And I *need* a dog and a pony.' She nodded curtly as she spoke, handing him another empty box to tear into flat pieces.

'And you think you'll get them if you pester her enough—is that the plan?'

'Mum? Yes.' Her nose wrinkled again. 'If it's not too expensive. We aren't rich.'

Kane smiled again at her matter-of-fact way of laying down the truth. But then he was enthralled by everything about her.

How could Rhiannon have kept all this from him for so long? She'd had no right to keep him from his child's first smile, first laugh, first step, first words—all of the things he would never get back or ever experience…

Even with only a few days of new-found knowledge, he couldn't ever remember resenting someone as much as he did Rhiannon. Hence he had chosen to stick closer to Lizzie since he'd moved in rather than allowing the tension that lay thick in the air when Rhiannon was around to *affect* Lizzie. At least on that one subject he could agree with her mother.

Clenching his jaw as a thought occurred to him, he forced nonchalance into his voice as he asked, 'Didn't your dad get you a pony or a dog before?'

'You mean Stephen?' She shook her head, a shadow briefly crossing her bright eyes. 'He wanted me to go to boarding school and said if I had a dog or a pony it couldn't go. But Mum didn't want me to go to boarding school. It's better when it's just me and Mum. And if we had a dog and a pony it would be *perfect*.'

Well, there was never going to be any problem getting information out of Lizzie, was there? That realization, along with the stunning sense of relief that washed over him that she had never called anyone else Daddy, brought a small smile back on to Kane's face. 'You always call him Stephen?'

'Yep,' She grinned as she lifted a pile of pony magazines out of a box. 'My mum called him Stephen.' She giggled and leaned closer to whisper, 'And some bad names too when she thought I couldn't hear her.'

Kane chuckled. Despite the fact that it was another subject he agreed with Rhiannon on—he had called Stephen plenty of names over the years. There was just something about him that had always grated on Kane's nerves.

With a large bag of ripped up cardboard in one hand, he followed Lizzie on to the landing. His smile was still in place when she turned to check that he was following her, slowing down to allow him to catch up with her when in reality he could have managed it in two strides.

It was thoughtful of her. She was an amazing kid.

'Do you have any kids, Kane?'

His breath caught at the innocent question. How in hell was he supposed to answer that one? It wasn't as if he could say,

Not that I knew of. And Rhiannon had made it very clear that she had never even hinted at it to Lizzie before. Damn her.

'Are you married?'

'You're just full of questions, aren't you?' He swapped the bag to his other hand. 'Should I call my solicitor before we go any further?'

Lizzie stopped at the top of the stairs, turning and frowning up at him as one small hand brushed back a long strand of hair from her face—hair the same colour as his, the eyes that were looking up at him the same colour as his. It was surreal.

'Why would you need to call one of them? Are you getting a divorce too?'

'No, I've never been married. It's in case you ask me anything I might get into trouble with the police for.'

Her eyes rounded. 'Have you been in trouble with the police, like one of those guys on TV?'

A loud peal of male laughter escaped to echo up and around the cavernous entrance hall. 'That would make me much more interesting than I actually am.'

'Well, I think you're interesting.' She smiled up at him, then turned and headed down the wide staircase.

'Thank you.' The sense of pride that gave him as he followed her grew exponentially.

'Stephen thinks you're interesting, he used to ask Mum tons of things about you.'

I'll just bet he did. Kane frowned briefly at the back of her head, forcing his voice to stay light. 'Stephen and I know each other from a long time ago; he was probably just wondering how I've been getting along all these years since I last saw him.'

Lizzie turned her head slightly as she got near the bottom of the stairs. 'What *is* a control freak, anyway?'

Kane blinked innocently. 'A what?'

'It's what Stephen said you are.'

'Did he now?'

She bobbed her head before turning on her heel and grabbing hold of the banister as she jumped off the second last step. 'And something about being over a bear.'

He quirked a brow as she pushed the door to the kitchen. '*Overbearing*?'

She grinned. 'Yeah, that and another thing about—'

'*Lizzie*?'

Both sets of eyes turned in the general direction of Rhiannon's softly demanding voice.

But while Kane surrendered to a swift wave of pure unadulterated resentment again—for the simple reason that every time he saw her he had an immediate, uninvited visceral response—Lizzie was quick to bounce on regardless.

'Oh, hi, Mum. We unpacked all the stuff for my room and Kane helped me tear up the boxes.'

'That was good of him.' Rhiannon glanced at the anger in his eyes before refocusing on her daughter, as if she saw her as some kind of shield between them. 'So what were you just saying to Kane?'

Lizzie shrugged. 'We were talking about Stephen.'

Kane watched Rhiannon's throat convulse as she swallowed, her eyes flickering up to his face and then away before she answered with a tightlipped, 'I see.'

Yeah. He'd just bet she did. Because she'd known from the start how little he thought of Stephen and yet she'd still gone ahead and married him *and* allowed him to become some kind of a stand-in father figure to Lizzie too. It was hellish hard to swallow.

His eyes narrowed when she looked back at him.

'Kane says they were friends from way back.'

Rhiannon's finely arched eyebrows rose, her brown eyes full of disbelief. 'Friends?'

Kane rectified the misconception in a flat tone. 'I said we knew each other.'

Lizzie looked surprised. 'You weren't friends?'

Forcing a smile in the face of such innocent curiosity, he added, 'Not exactly, no.'

'How come?'

He took a breath. 'Because we don't always get on with everyone we know.'

'Just like *you* don't get on with everyone in school.'

Kane glanced at Rhiannon again as she spoke, understanding immediately what she was doing but ignoring any hint of a rapport between them that that might have indicated. He was way past the stage of appreciating anything nice she might try to do, even if she was currently trying to smooth over a difficult topic on his behalf.

Lizzie sighed. 'Mum's still mad at me 'cos I pushed Sarah McCracken and she fell down.'

'Little girls don't go around pushing other little girls over.' Rhiannon glanced at Lizzie, then briefly up at Kane before concentrating on unwrapping a few more of the plates on the table in front of her, stacking them into a rapidly growing pile. 'Even when the other little girl says something they don't agree with.'

Wasn't finding it easy to look at him for long, was she? Kane smiled a small smile as he glanced down again, trying to keep all of his attention on Lizzie. Maybe her mother was starting to feel a little guilty? Well, she damn well should!

'What did Sarah say?'

Lizzie shrugged again. 'She said I only played football so that the boys would like me.'

He bit back a larger smile. 'And *do* you?'

'You want to watch she doesn't push you too. She may look all sweetness and light, but she has a temper.'

Like her mother used to have. Kane remembered the sometimes heated debates they used to have; he remembered how defensive she'd been about where she'd come from and how single-minded she'd been about making something of her life. And she'd managed it through a marriage into one of the oldest families in Dublin in the end, hadn't she? She'd traded up.

At the time it had made him glad he'd broken up with her when he had, even if he *had* maybe handled it badly enough for her to make the decision that he wasn't worthy parent material. After all, if she was only interested in marriage to step her into a safe financial environment it wouldn't have been much of a marriage, would it?

Knowing that made it easy now to damp down the memory of how much fun he'd once had making up with her after one of their 'debates'—long, languid sessions of making up. Until there had been a time when they had debated less and 'made up' more. At one time he had thought the memories would haunt him. But then she had married Stephen and he'd known he'd had a lucky escape.

All it had cost him was his daughter. And there wasn't a single doubt in his mind that she was his, now that he had spent time with her.

Lizzie giggled, the sound dancing around the room and drawing his attention back to her face. And instantly he smiled in response. For no other reason than it was what he always felt like doing when he looked at her.

'I'd need to grow a bit first before I tried pushing Kane over. He's *humongous*!'

'Nah.' He moved towards the back door with his bag. 'We office types are real weaklings. I'll bet you could push me over in a snap.'

Rhiannon watched him from below long lashes as he made the journey across the kitchen. *A real weakling, my backside*.

Her gaze moved slowly over his body, making the most of

what had once been an everyday sight. The man had always had his own particular way of filling a woman's eyes and the years hadn't diminished that any.

Not that he was handsome in a conventional Prince Charming way, oh, no. He'd never been that simple to peg. He'd always been, well, *sexy*, truth be told. Ruggedly handsome, definitely all male, and there was a sexuality to that that had been hard to resist, for her anyway.

It had been the first time in her young life that she'd met someone who could affect her on such a basic sensual level with just a silent gaze or half a smile. And the kind of passion they had eventually shared had been inevitable from the first day he'd looked at her. Damn him.

'That has to go in the recycle bin.'

Rhiannon watched as he glanced over his shoulder and flashed a brilliant smile at Lizzie, one that was open and honest, almost affectionate. And it tore off another piece of her heart when he answered with a brief salute and a, 'Yes, ma'am.'

Already father and daughter had an ease with each other, a rapport of sorts. And Rhiannon felt unreasonably jealous about that. Not for the way Kane was with Lizzie, but more for the way Lizzie was with Kane. She was still so innocent, so unbiased, so damn open and trusting.

'It's 'cos of the planet.'

'*Naturally.*'

Rhiannon rolled her eyes at the pun while Lizzie giggled. But the second Kane closed the door behind him he looked straight at her with such a look of venom that she almost called him on it. *Almost.*

But in a small corner of her traitorous mind she immediately wondered what it would take to be on the receiving end of the look he wore on his face when looked at Lizzie. Not that she wanted him to look at her with that kind of open warmth. It was just that she was very aware of the vast difference in the way he treated them.

Surely he couldn't entirely blame her for all of this? She wasn't the one who'd disappeared without a trace. And if he'd thought anything of her, which she'd believed he did once upon a time, then surely he couldn't have been so dumb as to not work out her baby was his!

All right, so she hadn't known she was pregnant when he had broken up with her, and he had been gone for a while by the time she did know—but even so!

Whatever it was that had pulled him off the face of the earth so completely must have been damn compelling!

His deep voice broke into her thoughts. 'Is there anything else that needs to be carried out?'

'No. But thank you for asking.'

'Can we eat yet?' Lizzie kneeled on one of the long wooden benches at the side of the huge table. 'I'm starved.'

'You're always starved.' She smiled indulgently. At least with her daughter she was on safe ground.

'Kane's starved too.' Lizzie nodded her head in his direction, her eyebrows hinting that he should back her up. 'Right, Kane?'

'I'm not sure I would use the word "starved".'

Again Rhiannon's gaze strayed across his body, moving over his flat stomach and then upwards to where his ribcage tapered outwards to his wide chest and broad shoulders, upwards still, until her eyes met his.

Kane smiled a slow smile in response, one that didn't make it all the way up into his eyes, allowing her to silently know he'd witnessed her study of him—and almost hinting at it being a victory of some kind.

Rhiannon immediately frowned with annoyance and looked away. 'I'm sure Kane doesn't want to be stuck with us twenty-four hours a day.'

'Oh, I don't know.' He allowed the words to come out in a low drawl. 'I think we still have a *lot* of catching up to do, don't you?'

She gritted her teeth. Damn him, 'You must have things of your own to do, phone calls to make to corporate headquarters, that kind of thing.'

Anything that would give her time alone with her daughter— away from his constantly stifling presence.

'No, I'm all yours.'

God, she hated him. 'Well, dinner won't be ready for a while and there's still plenty of unpacking to do.'

Which wasn't a lie; the removers had barely been gone a couple of hours.

'I'll cook.'

Her eyes widened in disbelief as she stared up at him again. '*You'll* cook?'

His face remained impassive. 'I've been known to beat an egg.'

He did look as if he was ready to beat *something*.

'It's really not necessary.' She hadn't actually contemplated them all sitting down to eat together every night. Was that seriously what he expected would happen? That they would sit around and play happy families while he was there?

'While you're still settling in, it makes sense if I throw something together. Lizzie can give me a hand while you're busy with something else. And anyway—' he smiled at Lizzie '—we wouldn't want Lizzie to starve to death, would we?'

Lizzie rubbed her stomach and sighed dramatically in response. 'I might be having a growth spurt, Mum. What would happen if I didn't get all the stuff I need to get tall?'

'You'd stay short.' She frowned briefly at Kane in warning. If he thought she was that easily dismissed he had another think coming. 'Really, I don't think you should have to cook for us. We can all respect each other's space while you're visiting.'

'Or we could just spend the time to get to know each other

after all these missing years.' He let the innuendo hang in the air like poison. 'Don't make such a big deal out of the odd omelette.'

'I'm not.' Which was a lie. She was, because it *was* a big deal. 'It's just setting a precedent is all—'

He remained deathly calm, folding his arms across his broad chest. 'Is it?'

'Yes, it is. The last couple of nights have been thrown together but if you cook tonight you'll expect me to cook tomorrow night and then we'll end up in some silly routine.'

'And that would be silly, why?'

'You're always saying the more people that share the work the quicker it gets done, Mum.'

Rhiannon ignored her own words of wisdom. 'We don't need to eat together every single night.'

And the last couple of nights had been hell. Every mouthful of food had felt like swallowing broken glass.

'Because it makes much more sense for us all to fend for ourselves—cook at different times—that kind of thing? Next you'll want a rota for the cooker and the washing-up.'

She mumbled her response without looking at him. 'I don't happen to think that's unreasonable.'

'Well, I think you're being silly. Don't you, Lizzie?'

Rhiannon wondered how much time she'd get in prison for a spur of the moment murder...

'Yup, I think you're being silly too, Mum.'

Rhiannon glanced at Lizzie's face. She was smiling, but already her perceptive gaze was moving back and forth between the two adults.

'Are you okay with helping him?'

Lizzie shrugged nonchalantly. 'Yup. But then that means we don't have to do the dishes, right?'

Rhiannon smiled down at her, glanced sideways at the studious expression on Kane's face and then bowed her head to concentrate on unwrapping more plates, a curtain of her long hair hiding her from him.

'All right, then. Whatever you're happy with, baby.'

Lizzie paused for only the briefest of moments before she answered with, 'W-ell, what would make me *really* happy is *a dog* and *a pony*…'

Rhiannon couldn't help it, she laughed at the ridiculous situation she found herself in. Then suddenly realized she wasn't the only one laughing, the sound of her own laughter briefly mixing with deeper male laughter.

When she looked at Lizzie, the child's mischievous blue-eyed gaze moved again between the adults before she laughed too.

Rhiannon looked upwards in time to catch the tail-end of Kane's open smile before he tore his gaze from hers and ruffled Lizzie's hair, his voice gruff but laced with affection.

'That's it, kiddo, never give up.'

He hunched down beside her to discuss what they were going to make for dinner, the words fading into the distance as Rhiannon stood transfixed by the sight of them side by side. They were just so very alike—the shade of their hair, the colour of their eyes, the way that Lizzie would tilt her head in thought.

And there it was again, that instant ease between them. So natural, so uncomplicated—*already*!

Another bubble of guilt rose up inside her. She had kept them apart all this time. And why, really? Because of her pride, because she'd been so very quick to decide he wouldn't want anything to do with his own baby? She could justify it by looking back at how much of a mess she'd been back then, how young and naïve and alone and scared—but even so…

Seeing them together now made her look back on the judgement call she'd made and, no matter how she tried, she found the decisions she'd made coming up shorter than before.

It wasn't a good feeling.

When Kane glanced up at her again, it took a moment for his face to come into focus. She blinked back the moisture at the back of her eyes, avoided his gaze and cleared her throat with a soft cough as she lifted the last plates off the table.

'I'll leave you two to it, then. I'll be in the library.'

Still avoiding looking at him, she walked out of the room with her head held high, determined to get away before she let any of her inner doubts show.

She might have just been forced to realize she may have made a huge mistake. But she wouldn't show it in front of *him*. Watching him with Lizzie was punishment enough.

Because she already felt as if she was losing her daughter a little to him. And that hurt beyond words.

CHAPTER FIVE

INSIDE a week Rhiannon was starting to cherish the time she had with Lizzie on the short trips to and from school. It felt like the only time they were alone, as if somehow she'd suddenly been thrust into a kind of competition for quality time with her daughter.

And she *hated* that.

It had been just the two of them for a lot longer than it had ever been with someone else in their lives.

And Rhiannon was discovering she preferred it that way.

Even the time when Lizzie was at school was tense. Because, though she managed to avoid Kane by focusing all her energy on unpacking and cleaning and adding the little familiar touches that would turn Brookfield from Mattie's house into a home that Lizzie could be happy growing up in, she was constantly aware that he was still there, even if he wasn't.

He disappeared again briefly at the start of the second week to conduct business back in Dublin, but he still managed to be back before Lizzie went to bed. And while he'd been gone a van-load of high-tech equipment had arrived, specifically, it felt, to remind Rhiannon that he hadn't gone for good.

She wondered just how long he intended the charade to continue. Because it honestly felt as if a little of her was dying every day. She'd never felt so alone. There was no one she could talk to about how she was feeling, not really, and where would she begin? After all, she'd learnt early in her life to cope alone and, much as she loved the few close friends she had, she wasn't going to phone them every second to talk it through when there was no point. They couldn't fix it.

Under different circumstances she knew she'd have talked to Mattie. But all that thinking that way did was to magnify the grief she'd been burying at the loss of her best friend. The grief she had hoped to work through by keeping busy at Brookfield and focusing on Lizzie being happy.

The latter goal was something Kane seemed to have taken off her hands, which left her working on Brookfield alone and finding reminders of Mattie at every corner. Increasing the sense of isolation in her own home, and making her more miserable with each passing day.

As it was what she considered her 'turn' to make dinner, she laid the table and checked nothing was burning before she went to seek out Kane and Lizzie.

It was only as she walked up the sweeping stairway to the second floor that she heard laughter echoing in the distance. And once again, surreally, there was deep, distinctly male laughter as well as the familiar melodic giggle that Rhiannon knew so well, the sound floating down temptingly from the third floor where generations ago the house servants would have lived.

It felt as if he was deliberately taunting her as she got closer.

'No way.'

'Yes way.'

'Then how does the Warrior Princess get past the monster? Quick, before I get killed!'

'Ah, now, a smart kid like you should be able to work it out. That's the whole idea.'

Gently pushing open the low door, Rhiannon's eyes took

stock of the room with a quick glance. At one time it would have been a dormitory; it was long and low, with four small windows sunk into the low eaves.

Except now it had a high-tech office suite in varying stages of construction, with flat computer screens, telephone lines and sheets of bubble wrap hanging out of cardboard boxes.

Well, he hadn't wasted any time marking out his territory, had he? With a frown, she vowed to ask him outright just how long he planned on staying.

Sitting in front of one of the large screens, where an animated flame-haired woman seemed to be working her way through some kind of magical maze of roaring monsters, was her enthralled daughter. And by her side was someone Rhiannon hadn't seen in years.

With ruffled hair curling adoringly against the back of his broad neck, wearing a plain navy T-shirt, faded jeans and beaten up trainers. Looking like he had used to look when he had been so very infectiously enthusiastic about everything life had to offer.

His deep laughter sounded again as Lizzie huffed in frustration at the game they were playing—*together*.

While Rhiannon stood alone in the doorway and felt the knife twist again in her stomach. She really didn't know how much more of this she could take.

So she scowled hard at what she could see of his profile, at the deep crease in the cheek she could see while her mind filled in the one on the other cheek that she couldn't. And even as resentment swelled in her chest again, so consuming that it almost stole away her breath, she *remembered*. She remembered afternoons with him, doing exactly the same thing with much more antiquated equipment. She remembered his excitement for the technology, the ideas, so far beyond her realms of comprehension, to make it better. How he would talk for hours about things that didn't make any sense to her, but she would listen anyway, just to hear to deep rumble of his voice and to see the sparkle in his eyes.

'Why can't I get her to go through that gap?' Lizzie let go of her control pad long enough to point at the edge of the screen.

He examined her profile, his eyes still sparkling in a reflection of her enthusiasm even as his tone of voice changed. 'Why don't we ask your mum?'

They both turned their office chairs to look at her, Kane's expression cautious again.

'Kane has some *really* cool games.'

'I'd heard that.' Cool games that half the world's children played on various pieces of equipment these days. She'd been surrounded by Micro-Tech goods for years, had tripped over magazine articles and seen his face on TV more than once. He was considered a technological wizard.

Rhiannon frowned briefly at him as she remembered how it had felt as if he'd been deliberately rubbing her nose in it with his success back then.

Then she smiled at Lizzie. 'Dinner's almost ready. Don't you think you should go get cleaned up and change out of your school uniform? I'm sure Kane has stuff he wants to do too. He doesn't need you up here disturbing him all the time when—'

'I don't mind her keeping me company.'

Rhiannon ignored him. 'If you have your homework done after dinner you can maybe play again for a while before bedtime.'

The concessions weren't getting any easier to make, but with each passing day she was finding herself making more of them without stopping to think about it as much. Probably because she was becoming more and more aware of the fact that Lizzie was flourishing under her father's attention. He always had time for her, listening intently to the things she said, helping her with her homework when she asked him to, explaining things in a way she always seemed to 'get'.

And although Rhiannon knew that, for Lizzie, he still held an element of 'new friend' novelty, she also knew with the instincts of a parent that it went beyond that for Kane. He was making up for lost time.

And there was that inner pang of guilt again.

One dark brow quirked the tiniest amount at how easily she had given up some ground, then Kane winked at Lizzie conspiratorially. 'C'mon then, kiddo. I'll give you a hand with your homework so you can come back quicker, okay?'

Rhiannon had to damp down the sudden need to drag Lizzie from the room while telling Kane in no uncertain terms that she had just as much right to that time with Lizzie as he did. Because, yet again, he had made her feel as if he had formed some kind of 'team' with Lizzie that she wasn't a part of.

She was turning into a shrew, damn him.

If she knew what it was he expected to happen once Lizzie knew who he was, that might help, because there wasn't going to be much more time spent putting off telling her, was there? Not when they were getting on so damn well.

Rhiannon just *really* needed to know what would happen next. Maybe then she could settle her mind.

Lizzie bounced out of her chair, oblivious to any of the undercurrents surrounding her. 'Okay, we have maths tonight anyway and you're way better at that than Mum is.' Oblivious to any angst the words may have brought her mother, she grabbed hold of his large hand and tugged. 'But I'm not sure about playing more 'cos Mum said yesterday I could get a pony and a dog, so I'll have to make a list of things to get for them.'

'Mum didn't say anything was definite,' Rhiannon softly chided while she stared at the small hand still held in Kane's larger one, the need to step over and separate them so strong that she had to grit her teeth together to stop herself from saying something out loud. 'She said we would talk about it some more.'

It had been the first thing that had put that same light into Lizzie's eyes she had when Kane was around.

Lizzie frowned. 'But Mum—'

'Animals are a big responsibility. Go get changed.' She unconsciously stared again at their joined hands.

As if somehow sensing it was a bigger problem than it actually was, and maybe even as a slight reflection of the concessions she'd been making for the last couple of days, Kane let go of Lizzie's hand and used the same hand to ruffle her thick hair.

'Go on—do as your mum says.'

It was the first time he'd backed up Rhiannon, even briefly. And it was an unexpected move. Her gaze automatically rose to lock with his, her shoulders relaxing when he didn't scowl at her in response. But she couldn't think of anything to say, all she could do was study him while he studied her.

Lizzie wrinkled her nose, then, quick as a flash, threw a huge smile up at him. 'Okay.'

Okay? Just like that? No more argument—from the child who, over the last few months, Rhiannon had had to debate and reason with over every little thing, sometimes for days? What in hell had he done to her?

Rhiannon moved to one side as she ran past with a call of, 'I'll be really quick. And then we can talk more about my dog and my pony at dinner.'

With a blink and a shake of her head, Rhiannon turned to go back downstairs. Sometimes being a mother just completely exhausted her, the subject of children's levels of energy still a mystery to parents worldwide, no doubt. But this immediate affinity with the father she had never met before was proving draining on a whole new level.

As was the constant physical awareness of where Kane was and the never-ending attempts her mind was trying to make at deciphering him. To, in some small way, sort out the memories from her decade-old perceptions and the present evidence in front of her eyes.

Rhiannon had always liked everything laid out in black and white—no grey areas. Grey areas held the unexpected. And the unexpected inevitably led to heartache in her experience.

She was at the top of the stairs when the skin at the back of her neck tingled again, the way it did every time he got closer to her.

'I'll make sure she doesn't play the game for too long. She'll be in bed at the normal time.'

'Thank you.' It was another small vote of support from him, which didn't go unnoticed. When he appeared in her peripheral vision, she glanced briefly at him, then down at her feet as they descended the first flight, telling herself she was just making sure she didn't fall flat on her face. But knowing it was because she was uncomfortable constantly looking at him.

'She's very bright.'

'Yes, she is.'

'And she picked up the game very fast for someone of her age. The target market is a few years older than she is now.'

'Her last school couldn't keep up with her computer skills. They reckoned she was at least two years ahead of where she should be. Her teacher even said there were times when she was able to explain how things worked before she was told how.' She frowned as a thought crossed her mind, then swallowed hard before saying it aloud. 'I guess she gets that from you.'

There were several heartbeats of a pause before he responded. 'Knowing there are things she gets from me must kill you, when you've spent so long hating me.'

The lack of anger in his voice surprised her, so she risked another sideways glance at him to confirm it and, for the first time in days, she found him looking back at her with more open curiosity, less resentment, and the distinct lack of a scowl, which knocked her back.

What was he playing at now?

When she faltered on the next downward step, a hint of a smile briefly quirked the corners of his mouth. 'Yes, I'm aware of how much you dislike me. You have to, to have kept her from me for so long.'

Rhiannon sighed. *Here we go again.*

'I'd convinced myself you didn't want anything to do with her.'

'Because I didn't answer the letter.'

'Yes.' She shook her head and focused on the stairs again, long wisps of her hair working free from her braid to brush against her cheek. 'Because you didn't answer the letter. I had no other way of contacting you. No one was able to get you on the phone, your room-mate didn't know where you'd gone or how long you'd be gone. We didn't exactly have a long enough relationship for me to have known your home address to send a Christmas card to your family, so the letter in your locker was the only thing I could think of.'

There. She couldn't make it any plainer than that, could she? And, in reality, she'd been pregnant before she turned nineteen. She'd wanted a solution from *someone*—where to go, how to support a baby, somebody to talk to when she had moments of panic about her ability to cope. If she'd thought he wanted to be there she'd have wanted that too because she'd needed him. And she'd *hated* him for not being there when she'd needed him.

Kane went silent again. And after a few steps Rhiannon couldn't resist glancing across at his face to see if she could see what he was thinking.

Unlike her, he was apparently confident enough in his own ability to make it down a flight of stairs without looking at his feet. Instead his gaze was fixed forwards, thick lashes flickering while he looked at the various paintings and wall-hangings as they appeared in front of him. But Rhiannon knew he wasn't thinking about anything he was looking at. He was considering what she'd said. And more than likely coming up with answering reasons for why she shouldn't have let it go at a letter when it had been something so important.

Well, he wasn't going to find anything that she hadn't spent the last few days torturing herself over. The thing was, she'd ultimately admitted to herself, whether she should have kept trying to get a response from him, either then or in the years afterwards, it didn't really make any difference. It was already done. And now she had to deal with the repercussions.

She fixed her gaze on her feet again.

'Did you know when I spoke to you that last time?'

'When you did the *thanks for the good times* speech?' She resisted the urge to look at him again.

But she could hear the frown in his voice. 'I didn't say that.'

A wry half smile worked its way on to her lips. 'I read between the lines.'

'Well, it wasn't what I meant.' This time the words were firmer, his deep voice low and unnervingly intimate as they continued down each step side by side. 'If it counts for anything, I spent a lot of time rehearsing what I would say to you.'

For no reason, Rhiannon felt a lump form in her throat. When really there was no need for her to be upset by his words. The only thing he had hurt at the time had been her pride, and maybe a little of the romantic notion any eighteen-year-old female possessed for her first 'serious' relationship. And it had to have been serious for her to have slept with him, but emotionally? Well, emotionally she had been fond of him, had cared about him. But she hadn't been in love. He hadn't broken her heart.

That had come later, when she'd had her lack of judgement regarding his sense of honour and responsibility thrown back at her. When she'd had to realize that he wasn't as great a guy as she had thought he was, which made her a gullible fool for even getting involved with him in the first place. Now *that* had broken her heart.

But not for long; she'd turned heartbreak into hatred pretty damn quick. 'You handled it as well as it could have been handled. No break-up is ever easy.'

'We weren't together all that long.'

'I know.'

'It was intense.'

A lump demanded she clear her throat before she spoke again. 'Yes, I remember.'

They crossed the first landing between the flights of stairs before he stepped in front of her. And, even though he didn't reach out to stop her the way he had so cavalierly those first couple of days, it was enough to get her attention, to make her chin rise so that she lifted her gaze to his eyes in question.

And for a long moment he just looked at her, his intensely blue eyes studying her openly before his brows rose in question. 'How much *do you* remember?'

Rhiannon's breath caught. He couldn't just ask her that! Let alone expect her to reply. What was she supposed to do—set aside all those years of resentment and anger so that she could hold a conversation about what a great sex life they'd had?

Over her dead, cold body.

The thoughts must have crossed her eyes before she could hide them because, before her incredulous gaze, he smiled. A slow, toe-curling smile that said he remembered as much about the subject as she did.

His voice dropped. 'I didn't mean that part.'

Rhiannon pursed her lips together, hating the fact that she'd just given him yet another small victory. 'All right, where exactly are you going with this, then?'

Glancing briefly over her shoulder to check that Lizzie's bedroom door was still closed, he stepped closer, his large body looming over her so she had to tilt her head back further to keep holding his gaze.

'I've had a few days to think—'

Oh, great. Now what?

His eyes searched hers and then rose to examine her hair for a moment before he locked gazes with her again. And Rhiannon had to swallow hard to loosen her throat, had to run the tip of her tongue across her lips to ensure she would be able to answer when he threw whatever he was going to throw her way, which drew his gaze down to study the simple movement.

He frowned in response. 'I wondered how much you remembered about the way I was back then. You had to have liked me well enough at some point for us to have—'

Rhiannon blinked in confusion. It wasn't what she had expected him to say. 'Of course I *liked* you. What a stupid thing to say. I wouldn't have—'

'Yes.' He nodded slowly. 'That's what I thought.'

With his body close again, Rhiannon was aware of a faint scent of coffee on his breath. And it occurred to her that he always had a scent of something that hinted at taste— cinnamon, peppermint, coffee. As if he were subliminally inviting her to sample those flavours.

She took a steadying breath. This was *not* going to happen to her all over again.

Kane took a breath, his gaze fixed on hers, his voice still deep, low and intimate. 'And if you liked me enough to get intimate with me *that often*, then you mustn't have thought I was all that bad a guy.'

She laughed sarcastically in response. '*O-oh*, I see where you're going with this.'

When she stepped sideways to get past him, he blocked her

again. 'Well, if you didn't think I was all that bad, then why did you think I'd have ignored your letter? That I'd have let you have my baby on your own? I don't understand that part.'

Rhiannon glanced nervously over her shoulder, making quite sure that Lizzie wasn't within earshot, but dropping her voice to a stage whisper when she looked back at him anyway. 'I was *eighteen*! I was eighteen and I was pregnant and you were the bloody *Invisible Man*! When you didn't answer I was too busy trying to hold myself together to try and understand why such a great guy had turned into such an ass overnight!'

'So you only hated me later, then?' He had the gall to quirk an eyebrow at her.

'Damn you!'

Having spat the words at him, she made the first move and grabbed hold of his wrist, dragging him behind her as she headed down the second flight of stairs.

A hint of amusement sounded in his voice. 'Nice to see that motherhood has mellowed you over the years…'

Feeling vaguely safer on the landing above the last flight, she released his wrist, glancing upwards again before she looked into his sparkling eyes.

'What do you want me to say, Kane?' She swung an arm out to her side while continuing in a slightly louder stage whisper than before. 'Do you want me to say that, despite everything I thought at the time, I was wrong? Then *fine*!'

The admission of guilt widened his eyes a little.

Rhiannon continued, her eyes filling up with the frustrated tears she had held at bay since she'd been forced to watch him with Lizzie. 'I've watched her with you and she's crazy about you. And you're equally as enamoured with her! And if you honestly think that I can love her as completely as I do and not feel guilty about her not having had that sooner—'

She paused to control her voice, which had begun to crack

on the words, looking past him while she fought back the tears, only briefly glancing into his astonished face before she gulped out, 'Then *you* have no better idea of the kind of person *I am* than I do of the kind of person *you are*.'

'Rhiannon—'

The softer tone to his voice tore the last shred of control that she had left, so that when she looked up at him again she could barely see his face for the wash of tears in her eyes.

And she *hated* that he was seeing that! So her voice broke on the admission while she pointed an accusatory finger at his feet.

'I would *never* have denied her her father because I know what it's like to have a father reject his child! So you're right, okay? And I was wrong. *You win*.'

CHAPTER SIX

RHIANNON disappeared upstairs before Kane had time to react properly, which left him standing on the landing between flights. If nothing else she was right about one thing; he didn't know her any better than she knew him.

His gaze rose while he frowned, pondering whether or not to go after her, to ask all the questions she had left him silently asking. But somehow he didn't think she would appreciate it if he did, because, even without any actual confirmation of his gut feeling, he just knew that to push her again at this point would be too much.

No matter how much he hated what she'd done, he still had to respect the fact that she was Lizzie's mother. *His child's mother.*

And, no matter how much he resented having his child kept from him for so long, he still had to show some respect to the woman who'd raised her so beautifully, especially now she'd admitted some guilt for the choice she'd made.

The problem was, her admission, delivered with so much emotion, made him think some more about his part in the wrongs of the past. Yes, he'd had his own reasons for not being there, for not telling her why he couldn't—

Like she'd her reasons for not telling him? He allowed, reluctantly, that that could well be the case. There was more to both sides of the story. But the only way he would know for sure if he was right about that was to get her to trust him enough to tell him and that involved an open line of communication, didn't it? Parents were supposed to be able to have that. Well, *good parents* were. If it just didn't involve getting to know Rhiannon all over again…

Truthfully, what he needed was a little time to mull it all over. *Again.* In between rapidly falling in love with his daughter, he'd already been mulling over a lot of things about her mother, and not coming up with too many answers—a fact that bugged the hell out of someone who had built his business on varying degrees of problem solving.

It was why he had pushed Rhiannon again. He needed answers. Because, as easy as it was to just stay angry at her, a part of him still needed to equate the Rhiannon he'd known before with the one in front of him in the here and now. To have purposefully kept his daughter from him for so long had been cruel—crueller than she could possibly realize—she *had* to have hated him. And yet she had done such an amazing job with Lizzie—how could that be? How could she hate him so much and yet shower so much love onto his child?

Was that just a mother's instinct? She'd already hinted at how much of him there was in Lizzie and, having spent time with her, he could see a lot of those things himself. Surely that must have been hard to see over the years?

So he'd pushed her to try and make sense of it and instead had been presented with even more to confuse him. He hadn't expected the response he'd got, and that was before she even admitted she'd been *wrong*!

It was talking about their previous relationship that had confused him this time. Or rather, how she had immediately assumed they were talking about the sexual side of it and how he'd had an immediate, powerful physical response to that. Damn her.

In her large, soft brown eyes he could see that she remembered every bit as much as he did about their time together. Standing alone in the hallway now, he wondered if she *knew* that he could still see so much in her eyes. Oh, she was better at disguising her thoughts than she'd been at eighteen, there was no doubt about that, which meant he had to search a little harder now for answers than he maybe had back then. But when he caught her off guard he could still see more than she probably realized he could.

It had translated into another thing to resent about her. Because it meant he had another reason to study her, to spend time *looking* at her, seeking out those thoughts in her eyes and trying to decipher them.

And somewhere in the last few days, he'd remembered it was something he'd always liked about her before. That very 'visible' intelligence she had.

Lizzie had it too. Her skill in picking up things quickly didn't come just from him. Oh, no. Having spent so much time with her, he now knew that there was an equal amount of her mother in her—probably more, because she'd spent all of her life with Rhiannon.

His head was really beginning to hurt.

A door opened on the landing above him and he stood tall, every nerve-ending in his body tensing as he waited for Rhiannon to reappear. But, when he looked up, Lizzie appeared at the banister, a grin on her face.

'Are you waiting for me?'

Kane exhaled and smiled back at her, the tension in him disappearing in a heartbeat. 'Yep. C'mon. Let's go get something to eat.'

Being in Lizzie's company was the only time he felt completely at ease in the house. But he couldn't keep putting off spending time with Rhiannon and he knew it. The line of communication had to be opened. He wanted answers. More than that—he wanted to know *everything* so that he wouldn't have to keep studying her and *noticing things*.

Like her natural ability to move gracefully, the sensuous way she would tilt her neck to rub her long fingers against her shoulders, how everything from the soft fall of her hair to that way she had of running the tip of her tongue over her full lips when she was nervous constantly reminded him of how innately feminine she was. And how that femininity would tug at an invisible part of him, the part deep inside that he hadn't felt so keenly in a long, long time around another woman.

If familiarity really bred contempt then he wanted that familiarity.

'I lit a fire in the stove room.' He stood in the kitchen doorway, studying Rhiannon with cautious eyes while he attempted to keep a soft tone to his voice.

She looked tired—dark circles under her eyes, her pale skin lacking its normal creamy glow.

And he'd grudgingly admired her guts for coming down to sit through dinner. No matter how she felt about him being there, she never let it affect the way she was around Lizzie. And that couldn't be easy, he *knew*.

Running a cloth over the end of the table, she focused completely on her task, taking a breath before she answered him. And that had to be tiring too, the constant caution around him in the brief moments when they were alone together.

He pushed his hands into the pockets of his jeans, leaning a shoulder against the door jamb. 'This place is draughty as hell, isn't it?'

'Yes, it can be. Most old houses of this age and size are, I think.'

All right, that had worked. So maybe talking about Brookfield was a starting point.

'Mattie said you always loved this place.'

'Yes.' She nodded, turning to rinse the cloth out at the deep Belfast sink. 'Brookfield is special. It's the kind of place you dream about when you're a little girl. I once saw a doll's house with three storeys like this place in a shop window and it became a dream house in my mind. And Lizzie has always loved it here.'

Kane thought back to the little he could remember of Rhiannon's life from before. And discovered he didn't remember much beyond the fact that her family hadn't been well off. Had she told him more than that? She couldn't have; he'd have remembered.

She spoke again. 'Where is she?'

Ah, okay, she was looking for her shield again, was she? And, with a quick glance at the set of her narrow shoulders, he could see that she wasn't happy with being alone with him again minus that shield. Well, if he was going to have to do without it in order to open a line of communication then Rhiannon was going to have to deal with it too.

'She went up to take her shower.' He pushed off the door frame and walked across to the Aga. 'Do you want coffee?'

He sensed her hesitation so placed an air of nonchalance into his tone. 'I'm making one anyway.'

'All right, then.'

Lifting the kettle from the back of the Aga, he stepped closer to Rhiannon at the sink to fill it with water. The minute his arm brushed hers, she jumped back a couple of inches and Kane sighed impatiently, studying her from the corner of his eye as he poured the water.

'I don't bite.'

She didn't answer him.

But she did fold the cloth, set it over the edge of the sink and step away from him to gather mugs and coffee from a cupboard.

Kane lifted the plate on the Aga and set the kettle on the plate to boil, before moving to the fridge to get milk. And in the tense silence it occurred to him that it was the first task they had worked on together, albeit in silent communication, since he'd come to the house. She'd stayed on the periphery while he spent time getting to know Lizzie, hadn't she? Not that he would probably have appreciated it any if she hadn't. But, even so—

'I think you and I should spend some time together before we tell Lizzie who I am.'

Rhiannon's eyes filled with disbelief. 'Why on earth would we do that?'

'Because I happen to think two parents who can work together is a better combination than two parents who spend all their time arguing. And we need to know each other better than we do now for that to happen.'

He set the milk carton down beside the mugs and tilted his chin a little to keep looking at her, his eyes searching hers to see what she was thinking.

She wasn't too enamoured with his idea.

And he smiled a little at that. At least he knew he wasn't the only one experiencing difficulty with it. 'We both know she's a bright kid. She's bound to feel the tension there is when you and I are both in the same room. And eventually that's going to lead to questions.'

Brown eyes searched his in the same way he had been doing with hers and Kane smiled a little more as he realized she was trying just as hard to read him. He doubted she'd be as successful though; he'd spent years learning how to keep his thoughts hidden from those around him; in private as well as in business.

Her eyes narrowed. 'You're saying we should get on better for her sake?'

'Yes.'

'And how exactly are we going to manage that?'

He shrugged a shoulder as the kettle bubbled. 'We liked each other well enough to make her together in the first place.'

A rose-coloured flush spread on her cheeks as she looked away from his face, focusing on spooning coffee into mugs. Her voice lower, she said, 'That was a long time ago. We were barely adults ourselves.'

'That's true. But surely, as adults, we should be able to find a way of getting on well enough to put Lizzie before ourselves.'

Her hand faltered and some granules of coffee spilt over the edge of one mug so she had to set the spoon down and retrieve the cloth to wipe them up. 'I don't see how we can be friends—we never took the time to do that before. It's too late now.'

'I don't think it's ever too late to make the effort to ensure our daughter doesn't feel like she has to bounce from one of us to the other.' He lifted the boiling kettle and carefully poured the hot water into each mug. 'Do you?'

As he filled each mug, she followed up by stirring the contents until the granules dissolved. 'I don't want her to feel she has to do that.'

'Neither do I.' He set the kettle back on the rear of the Aga and replaced the cover over the hotplate. 'That would be something we agree on.'

He turned and watched as she poured milk into the mugs, her long lashes flickering while she thought. And then he watched as she ran the end of her tongue over her lips, as her throat convulsed when she swallowed, as her small breast rose and fell when she took a deep breath. Then her face turned and she looked up into his eyes, the tiniest hint of a smile on the edges of her mouth as she handed him one of the mugs.

'Yes, I suppose it is.'

His mouth curled into a more relaxed smile. 'It's a place to start.'

Rhiannon took a long time to answer him. 'Maybe.'

His fingers brushed against hers as he took the mug from her, the touch brief but the sensation of it lingering on his skin even as she withdrew her hand and turned away, taking her own mug with her.

Wrapping his hand tighter round the warm mug, he studied its contents for a second, before his gaze rose and he saw her curl her fingertips into the palm of her hand as she walked away.

At the doorway she looked over her shoulder, taking another breath before she spoke. 'If the fire is lit then maybe we could all watch TV for a while before Lizzie goes to bed.'

It would be the first evening they all spent together and they both knew it. And, even with his fingers still tingling against the edge of the mug, something he would have added to his long list of things to resent only a few hours ago, Kane was nodding in agreement.

This had been *his* idea after all, hadn't it?

CHAPTER SEVEN

RHIANNON felt brighter after a few nights' uninterrupted sleep. And the fact that the stormy weather had subdued enough to let the winter sunshine flood through Brookfield's many windows lifted her spirits.

She still wasn't entirely comfortable with spending so much time in Kane's company, even with Lizzie there to act as a catalyst between them. But at least they weren't arguing. And that had to be a good thing. Kane was right; it would be better if they parented with better communication. She couldn't argue that.

It had been his use of words like 'we' and 'us' and 'together' that she'd had the most difficulty swallowing. Those words hinted at a bond between them that just wasn't there.

And yet, reluctantly, she knew it was. Lizzie was a bond that held them together whether Rhiannon liked it or not. At least now she didn't feel like so much of an outsider any more.

So, in the spirit of *entente cordiale*, she made two cups of coffee and then, with a deep breath, she made her way up to Kane's territory. She did, however, have a moment of indecisiveness before she knocked lightly on the half open door.

'...and then e-mail them to me.'

He glanced up, his mobile held to his ear, brows rising in question while she hovered in the doorway. Then his gaze dropped and he caught sight of the mugs in her hand ushering her in with a wave of his large hand.

'Yeah, that's fine. But I want Colm to look at the new graphics first; he knows the issues I had with the last lot.'

He leaned forward in his chair and reached for the one Lizzie normally sat in beside him, turning it round to face Rhiannon and inviting her to sit down with another wave of his hand.

But Rhiannon shook her head. She hadn't meant to interrupt him, or to sit down and actually drink the coffee with him. All she'd intended was to leave him the cup she'd made before she went down to look for the laundry there was bound to be in Lizzie's room.

When she went to set the mug on the desk beside him, he tucked the phone between his ear and his shoulder and took it from her hand, his other hand closing around her wrist, tugging her towards the chair.

He could even be bossy silently.

'Absolutely not, that packaging sucked. The whole idea is to have it look like a more expensive game, even when it's not.' He pursed his lips slightly when she resisted his direction and tugged on her wrist again.

So, with a roll of her eyes, Rhiannon complied, sinking down into the chair with a sigh. She could spare him five minutes, *she supposed*.

'Not before I see it.'

Blue eyes glowed warmly at her, no doubt another indication that he knew he had 'won' yet again, even on something so simple. But rather than scowl at him, she rested her weight on her toes and rocked the chair around to look at the screens behind her—one filled with images of an animated forest and another with lines of code that may as well have been Swahili to her.

'Yes—' she could hear the smile in his deep voice '—I did ring them.'

His low rumble of laughter drew her gaze back to his face as he rocked his own chair back and forth. 'Well, it must have been another query. No, you just never believe me when I say I did unless *you* put the call through.'

He laughed again. And, by straining her ears a little, Rhiannon heard the tail-end of the voice on the other end of the phone—a female voice. Well, that explained why he was in such a good mood.

'Okay, then, the next time they ring you can check and when they tell you I *did* reply you can call me back to grovel.' He grinned at whatever reply his female friend made. 'No, but you should. Okay. That'll do.'

He withdrew the phone from his ear, flipping the cover back into place with one long forefinger while he reached for his mug with the other hand. 'Thanks.'

'I was making one anyway.' She didn't want him making it into a bigger deal than it was. 'I didn't mean to interrupt. It can't be easy running your business from so far away.'

'It's all right, Sara keeps me informed; it's her job to keep me in line.'

Rhiannon had to force an expression of disinterest on to her face. It was none of her concern what woman kept Kane 'in line' these days, though it would be interesting to meet the woman who could manage it…

As if he had read her thoughts, Kane added, 'She's been my PA for three years.'

Rhiannon nodded, avoiding his knowing look by focusing instead on the images that were moving on the screen—the trees giving way to an open valley where tiny men were working, building houses and chopping trees. 'Is this a new one?'

'Nah.' He set his mug down, tossed his phone beside it and then leaned past her to click on the mouse, moving the image out so that she could see there was a world beyond the busy valley. 'It's an updated version of one of our best-sellers. Having some peace and quiet here has let me tweak it some.'

'Then I'd better let you—'

But he had his other arm across the back of her chair and used it to stop her from leaving. 'Have a go. I'll take you back to the set-up menu.'

'I don't know how to play computer games.'

'Well, considering how much Lizzie loves them, maybe you should learn.'

Nursing her mug between both hands on her lap, Rhiannon tried hard not to be so aware of how close he was sitting to her, his body creating a frame for her smaller one in the chair. Instead she focused on his profile as he concentrated on the screen, on the way his eyes moved back and forth, making sense of everything in front of him as easily as he breathed in and out.

Her gaze swept upwards, to the short gleaming strands of dark hair touching his forehead, one strand sitting in a different direction to the rest, as if he had run his fingers through it at some point.

And her fingertips itched against the mug, begging that she reach up and smooth it back into place.

Rhiannon frowned in annoyance—annoyance that she knew came through in the tone of her voice. 'I'm the kiss of death to anything electronic.'

She watched the slow smile form on his lips, his voice low. 'Yes, I remember.'

He glanced at her from the corner of his eye and out of nowhere Rhiannon found herself smiling in response to the sparkle of amusement in the blue depths. 'Well, if you remember then you'll hardly want me killing this one. Whatever you design these days is worth a hell of a lot more than anything I killed back then.'

'Yes, but anything I design these days is more user-friendly and better protected. If you manage to kill it, then I've not done my job right.'

He focused his gaze back on the screen while Rhiannon felt her breath catch in her chest at the memories that rushed uninvited into the front of her mind—as they had the day she had walked in and found him playing games with Lizzie. Maybe even stronger because it was just the two of them. She remembered the last day she'd 'killed' one of his creations…

He had stared in amazement that day, his mouth gaping, while the now outdated graphics had got tangled up with lines of code and Rhiannon had laughed her way through her apology. Until he had pulled her away from the screen and coaxed more laughter from her as he'd tickled his revenge from her ribs, the laughter eventually fading as Rhiannon found a way to 'make it up to him'.

She lifted her mug to her lips and swallowed a large mouthful of coffee to dampen her dry mouth, hiding her thoughts behind the rim.

'Right.' The arm that had been on the back of her chair snaked forwards while he forced his chair closer to hers so he could reach the keyboard. 'The idea is that you're the ruler of a new kingdom—you're shipwrecked—and you have to build an entire civilization from scratch using the resources you have at hand.'

His long fingers tapped at the keys. And beside him Rhiannon tried to focus on what he was doing, rather than the fact that his knees were now pressed in against the side of her leg or the fact that somewhere in her clouded mind she'd recognized he wasn't wearing the aftershave he normally did. He just smelled of soap, and shampoo, and that purely male undertone that was all him. And the simplicity of it reached out to the very core of her femininity, where it tugged, hard, until a dull ache formed.

How in hell could she still be physically attracted to him when she had spent a decade of her life hating his guts?

She glanced at the screen as he typed in a user name. 'Is that the game name you're giving me?'

'It's *your* name.' He glanced at her with an amused glint in the depths of his eyes.

Hell. If she was going to play the silly thing she may as well enter into the spirit of it. Anything other than being so very aware of him or running screaming from the room—the latter of which was hard to resist…

'Well, if I'm the *ruler* of this kingdom I think I'd be called something more interesting, don't you?'

'There's nothing wrong with Rhiannon.'

'I doubt you really think that deep down,' she mumbled as she set her mug down, nudging her chair forwards, her voice louder. 'I'll pick my own name.'

The wheels on his chair creaked as he moved back. 'Okay. Just follow the instructions on the screen.' Turning back to his own screen, he grumbled in a vaguely amused tone, 'And try not to kill it.'

It took a while for her to ignore the fact that he was still beside her, or at least be less aware of it as he worked in silence, but eventually the game demanded her attention and after half an hour she chuckled in amusement.

Kane turned towards her. 'What?'

Rhiannon shook her head while her fingertips directed another set of characters across the screen. 'Now I get why kids end up in front of these things for hours on end.'

When she glanced sideways at him he smiled in response. 'Addictive isn't it?'

'It's clever is what it is. There's something vaguely omnipotent, having control over all these little lives.'

'I could argue that the game also teaches you about trade and commerce, how to delegate, the importance of all forms of a society working together for the greater good of the whole…'

Rhiannon leaned back in her chair and eyed him with a combination of open curiosity and silent amusement.

Until eventually Kane shook his head. 'What's that look for?'

'All of your games are for educational purposes, are they?'

His chin dropped an inch as he smiled again, his gaze darting away from hers to the screen and then back into her eyes. '*No-o*, I wouldn't say that.'

'Hmm, 'cos I'd guess they'd be a harder sell to the kids if they were solely for educational purposes.'

'They probably would. But that doesn't mean every game doesn't teach something—even if it's just better computer skills or mouse dexterity.' He fixed her with an intense gaze, but not in challenge, in more of a sincere faith in what he did type of way. 'Computers are a part of everyone's lives these days, not like it was in the days when you knew me before and I was considered a geek for being as interested as I was. So it makes sense that some of the kids' leisure pursuits should have a grain of computer education in there somewhere. It makes it easier for them to prepare for the bigger stuff when they start their working lives.'

Deep down he was an idealist? Rhiannon wasn't overly surprised by that, even though it was at odds with the opinion she'd held of him for so long. But with every passing day she had to face up to the fact that her perceptions of him may have clouded her judgement.

The truth was she maybe didn't want him to be the things she'd liked then, because she didn't want to like him the way she had before. Even if liking him would make it easier to get along with him, which would in turn make it easier for them to make any parenting decisions—*together*.

And there was that word *together* again.

She searched her mind for something to say, dragging her gaze from the intensity of his blue eyes and her focus fell on the screen again, where her little kingdom was rapidly growing.

'Well, I'm glad Lizzie has you around to help her with this; it was always beyond me—still is, to a certain extent. She's already flourishing under your influence. She got a glowing report for her maths test.'

There was a long moment of silence before Rhiannon heard the leather of Kane's chair creak. From her peripheral vision she saw him leaning towards her, his voice a huskier rumble than before. 'I know. But thanks for that.'

Rhiannon silently cleared her throat, chancing a short glance sideways and then regretting it when she found him closer than she had realized, resting his elbows on his knees so that his face was level with her shoulder.

She shrugged, feigning nonchalance. 'I'm just being honest.'

'And we both need a good dose of that if we're going to find a way to make this all work.'

It was a scary thought. And there was that damn 'we' again.

'So, in the spirit of honesty—'

She gasped when he reached out over her lap, grasping hold of the armrest to turn her chair to face his so that their knees pressed tight together. Then he tilted his chin and looked up into her eyes. '—you did one hell of a job raising her, Mac.'

The old abbreviation of her surname hit her in the chest with silent blunt force. Oh, that was just playing *dirty*! No one but Kane had ever called her that. And at the time it had been a term of endearment—similar to darling or sweetheart.

Her heart beat erratically. 'Thank you.'

He smiled a soft smile that made it all the way up into his eyes, turning them into a deeper shade of almost cobalt blue. 'I'm just being honest.'

She smiled shyly back at him, because in that moment she felt *ridiculously* shy. As if she had somehow been transported back in time to when she had been a shy eighteen-year-old, swept off her feet by the twenty-one-year old student with the roguish smile and the irresistible sensuality. If anything he was more dangerous now. Back then she hadn't known just how compatible they were physically. But she knew now. Oh, yes. And she also knew it would be very easy to be swayed again.

The knowledge made her reach out for a defence shield. 'Well—' she wrapped her hands round both armrests and pushed back with her feet '—now that you've wasted lots of my time with your silly game—'

He grabbed hold of both armrests, lower down where they met the chair, and tugged her back again, the smile gone from his face. 'Don't do that.'

'Do what?' She blinked innocently. 'Leave? I have just as much to do as you do, you know. A house this size doesn't run under its own steam.'

'That's not all you're doing, though.'

How could he know that? 'What *am* I doing, then?'

This time his smile had the same cool edge to it it'd had from his first few days in the house, even though he softened it by using the same edge of sincerity from before. 'You're running away.'

Her chin rose. 'To all the laundry I have downstairs? Oh, please, it's tough to keep the enthusiasm at bay. Hold me back, do.'

'And now you're using sarcasm in defence.'

She scowled at him.

But he astounded her by chuckling in response. 'I remember more about you from before than you might like to think I do. But it's okay; I get it. This honesty thing doesn't sit any more comfortably with me than it does with you. So, if it helps any, you're not alone.'

She knew she was staring at him, but she couldn't stop herself from doing it.

So she saw when his gaze rose to her hair, how it followed the waves down the side of her face, over her shoulder, to where the tips grazed her breast. Then it rose, slowly, pausing on her mouth for a moment longer than it had anywhere else, before his thick lashes rose and blue locked once again with brown.

He was frowning by then. 'We might not be happy about it. But we'll have to learn to be honest with each other, for Lizzie's sake.'

Rhiannon nodded dumbly, echoing his words in a monotone as he released her chair and swung back to his screen. 'Yes, for Lizzie's sake, I guess we do.'

There couldn't be any other reason. Not again.

CHAPTER EIGHT

IT WAS the largest dog she had ever seen.

Rhiannon's eyes widened as it stood with its huge head at her waist level, sad dark eyes staring up at her while long silvery threads dropped from its huge jowls all over the slate floor of the kitchen.

She swallowed hard, afraid to move in case it, well, *ate her*. She doubted it'd even need to chew.

'Isn't he gorgeous?' Lizzie grinned from the doorway. 'Kane let me pick and he had the bestest droopy eyes. His name is Winston.'

His name should have been Godzilla. 'This is *your* dog?'

'Uh-huh.' Lizzie skipped over to wrap her arms around the animal's thick neck. 'My very own dog. I'm gonna make him a bed to sleep on in my room.'

The hell she was. 'And *Kane* got him for you?'

Without consulting her? Oh, he was pushing his luck wasn't he? What had happened to *communication*? So much for letting the two of them loose for an afternoon on their own. 'Where *is* Kane?'

'He's taken John, you know, John who has ponies—round the back to look at the stables.'

Oh, had he, indeed?

Sidling gingerly past the largest dog on the planet, Rhiannon yanked open the kitchen door and walked out into the cobbled courtyard at the back of the house, taking a moment to listen for voices rumbling from the old stables that had once housed the carriage horses and hunters in days gone by. Yes, it was a sin to see them empty and unused, but that didn't mean that Kane could just hop out and fill them with a menagerie of animals at Lizzie's request.

Not without at least discussing it with Rhiannon first. Was she going to have to debate *every* tiny little detail with him?

Following the low sound of male voices, she then leaned inside one stone archway, her arms folded across her breasts while she eavesdropped on their conversation and allowed her disobedient eyes to rove over Kane from head to toe while she could do it unnoticed.

What she saw brought a smile out to twitch at the corners of her mouth. Because he was making quite an effort to fit in with country life—finely checked shirt, another pair of jeans and even heavy work boots on his large feet.

But she'd be damned if she found the fact he'd made any effort at all either endearing *or* sweet. He was Mister Corporate Big Shot now; he didn't belong in the middle of nowhere.

'A few thousand should pick you up something safe all right. But they do better in company.'

Kane was nodding. 'Well, there's plenty of room.'

And on that note she cleared her throat, making her presence known as she unfolded her arms and pushed her shoulder off the wall. 'Do I get to join in this conversation before you turn Brookfield into a zoo?'

Ignoring the all too familiar blue eyes that focused on her as she approached, her skin automatically tingling in awareness, she instead fixed her attention on the younger man at his side. 'Hello, John. It's nice to see you again.'

'And you, Rhiannon. You're looking grand as usual.'

She smiled a genuine smile at him, the sight of his openly friendly face a welcome break from the one she had to physically force herself not to look at. 'You're still the charmer, John. How's your dad?'

'Ah, sure, he's as much of a terror as always. He needs you to come up and soften him up. A visit from you and Lizzie always brightens him up.'

'We'll take a run up to see you soon, I promise.'

'Do now.' John winked at her. 'We can take the horses up into the forest this time.'

She laughed. 'Only if I get something half-dead.'

'Don't I always look after you?'

Kane's voice held a barely disguised tone of disapproval. 'You've obviously met before. John is here to check out the stabling for a pony or two.'

Or two? She quirked an eyebrow up at him, refusing to be put off by hooded eyes or the tight line of his mouth.

'We can have a talk about that—there's no hurry.'

'I told Lizzie I'd get her one.'

Rhiannon smiled sweetly, her voice coated with sugar as she practically purred back at him, 'I think the dog is a big enough gift for one day. And I do mean big. Weren't there any smaller breeds—Irish Wolfhound or maybe a baby elephant?'

John laughed while Kane managed a thinly disguised glare at him. 'Danes are known for their loyal and friendly nature. Winston's a big softie.'

Rhiannon nodded sagely. 'With emphasis on the big. Couldn't she at least have had a puppy?'

Kane eyes suddenly sparkled. 'He *is* a puppy.'

Her eyes widened. 'That thing is going to *grow*?'

John hid his second burst of laughter behind a cough, reaching a hand out to pat the iron bars that enclosed the top half of the stables. 'Well, it's certainly all still sound enough in here if you do decide to get a pony for Lizzie. Sure give me a call when you're ready and I'll keep an eye open for something that might do.'

'Thanks, John.' Rhiannon smiled again, reaching her hand out to shake his larger one as he stepped forwards. 'Send my best to your dad.'

'I'll tell him you'll be up to visit soon.'

'Do.' And she was still smiling after his tall, lean figure disappeared out through the same archway she had come through. Until, out of the corner of her eye, she saw Kane move to stand beside her, his arms folding across his broad chest, and she immediately felt the air change, every nerve-ending in her body coming to life.

She took a deep breath and waited, her gaze still fixed forwards while she listened for the steady sound of his breathing. And she didn't have to wait long for his deep voice to resonate.

'He's not your type.'

When she turned her head, she discovered he was tilting his head towards her, his eyes carefully studying her expression, waiting for her reaction. As if he would gauge his response by hers.

Lord, but he was tempting—physically speaking, of course. Up close, even when he was being all determined and forceful, there was just a delicious, very sexual intensity to him.

She damped her lips with the end of her tongue, taking her time to word her answer as the tingling awareness sparked like static electricity when his eyes focused briefly on her mouth. Maybe subliminally a part of her knew she would get that reaction when she did it?

Rhiannon sincerely hoped not; she didn't want to encourage him. But apparently she couldn't help herself. 'And what exactly *is* my type, then?'

His gaze rose swiftly, dangerously glinting eyes locking

with hers, narrowing briefly before he answered with a firm, 'Not him. You'd run rings round him.'

Not that she was actually planning on dating in the near future, but even so… 'You don't know that.'

The smile was slow, oozing with self-assurance. 'Actually, yes, I do.'

Rhiannon rose to the bait. 'So you're going to pick out my boyfriends as well as deciding how many million animals I'll have to care for after you leave?'

'Lizzie wants a pony, you know that as well as I do, so I'm getting her one, and I'm not going anywhere yet so the boy-friend thing isn't an issue.'

Meaning he would have a problem if she did date someone else under his nose? She wasn't sure she wanted to know the answer to *that* question.

So she tried to focus her mind on the pony issue instead, studying his eyes for a long time while a realization slowly grew inside her mind. 'Surely you're not planning on buying your way into her good books? You don't have to do that; she's already crazy about you.'

Seriously—was that what he thought being a father meant? Oh—he had a lot to learn, didn't he? And she couldn't believe he still felt he had to do that.

How could he not see how much Lizzie already cared for him? And frankly, having seen so much of them together of late, Rhiannon couldn't blame her. He had a gentleness about him when he was with her, looked at her without the smallest attempt at guarding his feelings—feelings that already ran deep. Certainly fathoms deeper than anything he had ever felt for her mother, which had hurt, in some strange way she'd chosen not to investigate further.

But he was still on a crash course in fatherhood, wasn't he? She hadn't known herself what parenting meant before she had

Lizzie, and she was still learning, every day. Even so, the reasoning astounded her. By buying her expensive gifts—granting Lizzie everything her heart desired—did he honestly believe he could get her to love him more?

'So everything she mentions she'd like, you're going to get for her? Just like that? Kane—' Her voice softened a little on his name, as if she was trying to convey that she understood why he was trying that method of inducement, even when it was the wrong way to go.

He frowned hard. 'So now I can't buy my own daughter presents?'

If it was at all possible, he stood a little taller, towering over her in a way that once again made his presence imposing and domineering. He fell back on that method a lot these days. And Rhiannon would bet that not too many people crossed him because of it.

But she didn't back down; instead, as usual, lifting her chin the extra inch to compensate. After all, they'd been making the effort to get on better of late, and if he remembered as much about her as he claimed to…

'That's not what I meant and you know it isn't. It's just better if she continues falling for you because of you rather than for what you can get for her, don't you think?'

Heaven alone knew it was why she'd ended up with him herself. And there were still the very odd moments when she was reminded of that while he was around.

The nod was very brief, his eyes warming a little as he studied her, before he glanced to one side and Rhiannon was momentarily distracted by the faintest breeze that lifted the finer hair against his forehead.

It was becoming an obsession, that hair of his. Again. She had used to love touching his hair, and it was probably why her fingers had itched that day in the office. Always, when they had sat in front of a computer screen or watching television, her hand had inevitably ended up at the nape of his neck, her fingertips absentmindedly moving from the shorter, coarser strands that touched his warm skin, to the slightly longer, smoother strands against the back of his head, where they would thread into the thickness.

It had been the simplest of physical contact really. But when he was tired, he would lean back into that touch, his lips would part as he sighed in relaxed contentment. Sometimes his head would turn and when his firm mouth moved across hers her fingers would thread deeper into his hair, willing him closer.

How had she forgotten that? Maybe, simply because she hadn't *wanted* to remember.

He took a deep breath. 'I still feel like I have ten years' worth of presents to make up for—Christmases, birthdays, all that. A pony and a dog don't seem to me to be that much in the great scheme of things. I'm not trying to buy her affection.'

When he turned away Rhiannon felt a bubble of disappointment grow in the pit of her stomach; it felt as if they had just taken a step backwards. And she really didn't want that to happen.

It left her floundering for a way back to where they had only just tentatively managed to get. And only one question came into her mind—the one that had been causing her the most headaches of late from trying to find an answer on her own.

Because there'd been a catalyst for her reactions all those years ago; that initial action that had driven her to make the choices she had, even though she now knew they hadn't been the right ones. And the guilt she now carried drove her to want to understand why he had disappeared when he had. The need to know growing exponentially, day by day, to almost consume her as she got to know him all over again.

And there was only one way to find an answer, wasn't there? So the question jumped out.

'Why did you disappear?'

Kane stopped suddenly. As if an invisible wall had appeared in front of him. Then his head turned and he looked over his shoulder, his eyes focused on a point on the ground in front of her feet. 'When?'

'You know when.'

'It doesn't really matter now. We're making an effort to fix things. Let's just let it go at that.'

She followed him when he stepped away again, her voice low. 'I don't think I can. I can't go back and change things. But every action has a reaction. Maybe I might have pushed harder to make sure you knew if you'd been remotely in the area of approachable.' She laughed a nervous laugh, fully aware that she was rambling. 'But you were some kind of ghost that was there one minute and gone the next. It was like you didn't even exist any more until you formed your company and made the announcement to the press with Mattie. Lizzie was almost three, then.'

She stopped when he stopped and then took a deep breath, forcing herself to stop rambling long enough to make sense of what she was trying to say.

'So now that I know I made a mistake not finding you to tell you, I need to know. Where did you go in those missing years? What made you drop out of Trinity early?'

Kane looked over his shoulder again. A muscle in his jaw flexed, his gaze shifted from her face to focus on a random point on the stone wall beside him. And in that instant, the minute movements told Rhiannon that, whatever it had been, it was something he still wasn't entirely comfortable with.

Thick, dark lashes flickered slightly as he searched the wall, taking the time to decide whether or not to answer her most likely. So Rhiannon tried again, feeling distinctly as if she were walking on eggshells as she braved another step closer to him, to where it would have taken very little effort to reach out and touch him.

Instead her arms hung redundantly at her sides, her cold fingers flexing in and out of her palms while she bit down on her bottom lip, willing him to give her a reason to understand, to complete the picture.

She really needed to know because, for her, it was the missing part of the puzzle. And it might only have been a moment or two longer while she waited for him to answer, but it felt like an eternity.

And still he seemed to be struggling inwardly. So Rhiannon tried to make it easier. 'I need to know.'

His gaze flickered briefly in her direction again, dark brow quirking, possibly in reaction to the somewhat breathless sincerity in her voice.

'It doesn't really matter any more, does it? We both made decisions then that we could have had no idea would stretch forward this far.'

The fact that he was trying to share the responsibility for the mistakes that'd been made softened a part of her she'd been protecting since he'd reappeared in her life. But it also made her need to know even stronger.

'It matters to me.' Rhiannon realized she had barely spoken the words aloud, so she cleared her throat. 'The reasons I had for doing the things I did then still matter to you, don't they? So why should your reasons be less important to me? It's all part and parcel of the same mess.'

'Maybe.' His voice was equally as soft, held a husky edge that drew her step closer to him. 'But I've been thinking some and what I think is that knowing doesn't change anything. And we're starting to make some progress, I think. Not arguing was a step in the right direction. And we agreed—this isn't about us—it's about Lizzie.'

'Yes, it is.' She knew he was right about that—there was too much water under the proverbial bridge. 'But I still need to know.'

He turned away, forcing Rhiannon to look at the back of his head. So she sighed and tried one last time, silently promising herself it *would* be the last time; she couldn't keep showing how much it still mattered. Because he was right about that too—it *shouldn't* matter any more.

'I've watched you with her, Kane, and the way you are reminds me of the way you used to be. You're right; I didn't hate you when we were together. And I don't want to carry around all the hatred I had for you afterwards any more either. But when you left and I found out I was pregnant, I was scared. And there was no one for me to talk to about that because the father of my baby was gone. I got through it on my own, but I don't think I ever forgave you for that.'

One last step and she was right behind him, her eyes focused on the short strands of hair against the column of his neck. 'I'd really like to understand it all so I can let it go. That's all.'

'Just like that? I tell you why I left and you put aside ten years of hating me? You have a tight control on your emotions, don't you, Rhiannon?'

She could hear the disbelieving edge of sarcastic humour to his deep voice. It was the last straw. She had tried. And, no matter what thoughtful, humorous, warm or even sensual roads he made into her psyche from here on in, she would burn in hell before she'd hold out an olive branch to their past again.

So she sidestepped around his massive frame and mumbled on her way past, 'Don't ever say I didn't try.'

She was almost through the arch when his voice sounded again, low, deep, rumbling, but with a flat matter-of-fact tone, so that she knew he still wasn't happy with telling her the truth. 'I was sick.'

Rhiannon froze. Without thinking about it, she found herself doing exactly what he had done only a matter of moments before—focusing on the stone wall, staring at the old cobwebs that had woven along the concrete lines within the irregular surface. While the words echoed inside her brain.

Like some kind of cruel cosmic echo of the day that Mattie had said, *'I'm sick.'*

'Sick—how?'

She forced her heavy feet to pivot round so that she could search his face for the same fatalistic expression Mattie had worn that day. And Kane's eyes rose to lock with hers, the blue so dark across the distance between them that they looked as black as they had that first night in the kitchen.

He shrugged his broad shoulders, his hands pushing deep down into his pockets again. 'Sick enough to have to go and make the time to deal with it.'

Tilting her head to one side, she tried searching his face for the information she couldn't get from his eyes. 'What kind of sick?'

'Not with anything you could have caught—if that's what you're worried about.'

Damn, but he could be cruel when he wanted to be!

'That wasn't what I meant.'

Maybe it was the way she choked the words out, maybe it was simply the fact that she was staring at him with such wide eyes. Whatever the reason, his shoulders relaxed a little.

But he still glanced away before clearing his throat and saying what she had prayed he wouldn't say. 'A form of cancer.'

No!

He must have read the anguish on her face because he immediately made an attempt to negate it. 'I've been in remission for a long time.'

Slowly, so very slowly, little snippets of memories rose inside her head to form a different picture.

'That's why you and Mattie suddenly became such good friends.'

They had been friends in university, but not in the same way they had been maybe four or five years after. It was the same way all over the world, she had reasoned—networks of friends forming because of their ties to one person and not necessarily because they got on with the whole ensemble. But, even though Rhiannon had always wondered why the relationship had changed, she'd never sat herself down to figure it out, until now.

'You had something in common.' Mattie had fought leukaemia for most of his short life.

'Yes.' A dark frown creased his forehead again. 'Except that I won and he lost.'

And he actually sounded as if he felt guilty about that!

Rhiannon felt as if her world had tilted beneath her feet. Everything she had thought she had known—everything she had judged him on—

'He knew that was why you left when you did.'

Kane stepped closer to her, while Rhiannon's gaze dropped, focusing on the smattering of dark hair she could see peeking above the V of his shirt.

'Not until he got sick again a few years back, no. He knew the truth about Lizzie too, didn't he?'

Rhiannon nodded. 'Yes.'

'I thought he had to have.' He shook his head, a wry smile on his mouth. 'I should have worked it out for myself. It's something that's been driving me crazy this last while. I *should* have worked it out.'

'No, I should have found you and told you. If I'd known—' She flung one of her redundant arms out to the side, then lifted both arms and wrapped them around her waist, squeezing in tight. 'Why didn't he tell me you were sick?'

When he didn't answer her gaze rose, and when she was finally looking into his eyes he smiled, his gaze softening in a way that reminded her again of the way he had been with her before.

She'd been so very wrong about him, hadn't she?

'If I had to take a guess I'd say that you weren't any more prepared to allow him to tell me than I was to let him tell *anyone* I'd been sick.'

He was right again—about her, anyway. The first time Mattie had asked her outright if Lizzie was Kane's, she'd made him promise never to bring it up with Kane. *Ever.* Or she would *never* forgive him. As her best friend, he had respected that— argued it, but respected it.

As far as she'd been concerned, she'd made the effort. She'd known *exactly* why she'd done the things she had, or rather, had convinced herself she had.

But *Kane*, wait a minute— Her eyes widened in question. 'You didn't tell *anyone*?'

He shrugged again, as if he was discussing the damn weather. 'My immediate family knew. But making it public knowledge wasn't exactly the best plan when setting up a new business and trying to attract investors. I wouldn't want shareholders to know now either.'

'But you said you were in remission.' Having hated him for so long, she was stunned to the core by the flash of excruciating pain that cramped across her midriff. She wasn't sure she could go through that again with someone she cared about.

She frowned hard. 'Are you saying—'

Varying emotions crossed swiftly through the blue of his eyes, but were immediately hidden with the unreadable, hooded gaze that she was all too familiar with. 'No, I'm not. I've been clear for eight years. But the word cancer has a tendency to strike fear into the people who have money invested in you. That's all.'

Not to mention the fact that they looked at you differently. Mattie had made jokes in private about it, but Kane wasn't that type. Anything he felt ran deep. And the changes in him from when she had known him before made more sense with her new found knowledge. He'd shut himself off, had disappeared from the world, had dealt with it alone—had learnt how to hide his thoughts and emotions from the people around him.

And Rhiannon understood that, maybe better than most. The immediate rapport with Lizzie, the open affection, the complete honesty he had with her—the very things she had been so jealous of—had only made her feel so alone because she so badly needed to be all of those things with Lizzie too.

The realization must have shown in her eyes because Kane frowned in response. 'Thanks, anyway, but I don't need your pity, Rhiannon. I was sick; now I'm not. End of story.'

For all the times he had read her correctly, he was way, way off base with how she was feeling this time. 'I'm not—'

'Yes, you are.'

No, not in the way he thought she was. It wasn't pity; if anything, it was a new found understanding and respect. If she had known back then what she knew now…

Kane took a deep breath, his shoulders rising again as he dragged his large hands out of his pockets. Then he stepped closer and Rhiannon held her breath while she waited to see what he would do next.

She almost sighed as she breathed in the cinnamon scent of him up close. She almost closed her eyes as his closeness overwhelmed her.

He leaned his head in a little, his breath stirring the hair against her neck while he focused on a point past her ear. 'So now you know. As to the spoiling Lizzie issue that we started this with, you'll have to get used to it for a little while. But I'm not trying to buy her affection.'

Rhiannon turned her head slowly, tilting her chin upwards at the same time in one fluid motion so that she could look into his eyes up close. But when she did, she couldn't seem to find words, even ones to reason with him on the subject of spoiling

Lizzie. All she could do was stare, as if she was suddenly seeing him for the first time.

Kane's eyes studied her in a similar way, his gaze rising to sweep over the hair against her forehead, over each of her arched eyebrows, from one eye to the other.

And Rhiannon couldn't breathe. She couldn't remember ever wanting someone to kiss her so badly.

But his thick lashes merely brushed against his tanned skin a couple of times before he spoke in a husky whisper. 'I do want her to love me of her own free will. Of course I want that. What father wouldn't?'

'She already does.'

'I hope so. She's the only child I'm ever likely to have, thanks to the cancer.'

CHAPTER NINE

THEY slipped into a routine; one nowhere near as dreadful as Rhiannon had once thought it would be, but not completely comfortable either. Because fairly soon she was all too aware of the fact that she had gone back to relying on Lizzie as a shield.

And that just wasn't right. She should be able to have at least *some* kind of relationship with her child's father, shouldn't she? It had even seemed possible for a fleeting moment—tentative maybe, but a place to start. And true, she was discovering there was much more to like about him than hate, but she still couldn't let herself relax when he was around.

So each day became some kind of test, with a whole new set of thoughts and feelings for her to resolve. She would watch him when he couldn't see her doing it, she would listen carefully to his voice when he spoke, would try to put all the pieces of his personality together so that he made sense to her, all the while so very *aware* of him. Because her nerve-endings would tingle with anticipation when he walked into the room, her pulse would skip through her veins every time his body was close to hers, she would smile without stopping to think about it when he laughed, and most of all her heart would twist when he let his guard down with his child and his affection for her shone in his blue eyes.

Maybe because she now knew that this child he cared so

much for might be the only one he ever had and that broke her heart. Lizzie was so amazing—not that her mother was at all biased, of course—but the thought of her being the only one of her there would ever be…

It was almost too painful to think about. Not to mention being too *confusing* to think about, because it'd never occurred to Rhiannon to have another child after Lizzie, and she wasn't sure she wanted to know why she was suddenly so obsessed by the thought of another one.

But none of that was anywhere near as consuming as the ache she felt when she thought of Kane having to fight a battle with his illness alone. If she'd been given the choice, even without love to bind them together, she now accepted that she'd been attached enough to the young man he'd been to have wanted to be there. *Through all of it.*

So although only recently she'd been jealous of the time he spent with her daughter, she now found she was jealous of Lizzie's time with *him*. And that was unreasonable as hell from the woman who hadn't been able to stand in the same room as him until very recently.

But she hadn't known then what she knew now.

Meanwhile, *he* had slipped into his role as Lizzie's father as if he'd always been there. He liked taking turns doing the school run, he loved her chatter in the car when they were together and how she would run out through the gates to tell him about her day. He liked spending time doing homework with her, he loved being astounded by her intelligence and her ability to problem solve—the latter another reminder of something he was good at himself. And Rhiannon knew all those things from the chatter around the table at night, which was the time *she* loved the most.

She loved it because they would all sit together in the warm room as Lizzie bounced the conversation back and forth between them all, forcing Rhiannon to laugh out loud when she knew she would have felt awkward letting go that much if it was just Kane there. But even that special time was laced with a bitter sweetness—allowing her a small glimpse of what family life could be like if he was a permanent feature, if things were *different*...

So, in between sharing the daily tasks, Rhiannon launched herself wholeheartedly into learning about the intricacies of running a house the size of Brookfield. It kept her mind focused for a few hours each day when their 'buffer' was at school. It was important, she told herself. After all, Kane would be gone soon but Brookfield would remain, even if her owning Brookfield and Kane owning the estate tied them together all over again. Apparently there was no escaping him.

She grew restless after lunch, piles of papers all over the desk in the library testimony to the fact that she still had a long way to go to make sense of everything. And when her head started to ache, she knew she needed a break. It wasn't raining, so she took herself out for a walk to clear her head.

But she didn't get further than the courtyard at the back of the house before she heard a rustling from the stables, where she found Kane.

He had his shirtsleeves rolled up while he threw bales of straw down and then shook them loose. And, mesmerized, she watched the muscles in his forearms moving, watched as he bent down every so often to lift a section that wasn't quite loose enough for him to fork out, while her nerve endings tingled with the familiar sensual awareness.

It was the first time she'd been completely alone with him since she'd made herself so purposefully busy. And a part of her knew she'd be safer just walking away, but she couldn't seem to do it.

'Lizzie will kill you for doing that without her.'

He looked up in surprise, a broad grin immediately forming on his face. 'She'll forgive me when we go get the stupid beast.'

The stupid beast that had been his idea, but Rhiannon had eventually allowed—the one that he'd at least consulted with her on when it had come to the actual selection, which hadn't gone unappreciated. And honestly, if it settled into daily life as well as Winston had, then it would be fine. Though Rhiannon sincerely hoped she wouldn't end up with a pony trailing round the house after her in Lizzie's absence. Not that a pony could be that much larger, realistically.

'You do know she has you wrapped round her little finger, right?'

'Only because I let her think she does.'

The words drew forth an unguarded burst of disbelieving laughter. 'Liar.'

He grinned again. Oh, yes, now she remembered—*this* was when she liked him best, when they could just hold a conversation without there being an undercurrent. Why couldn't he be like this all of the time?

'Be nice now—especially since it just so happens I've been thinking about you.'

Rhiannon's eyes widened.

He continued. 'I was thinking that a computer system for the household accounts might make your life simpler. Lizzie said you had a ton of paperwork.'

And now he was being thoughtful on *her* behalf? *Wow*. What had brought that on? She dropped her gaze briefly to the toe she was using to absentmindedly push loose straw back into the stable. 'It would, actually—I'm going cross-eyed.'

'All right, good.' He grinned again. 'Not to the cross-eyed part, you understand. I'll find someone who can set something tailormade up for you.'

She couldn't help but tease him. 'Are you saying you're too expensive for Brookfield?'

'Well—' he cocked his head to one side, lifting his foot to

rest on the pitchfork '—that *is* true, as it happens. But I was thinking that someone closer by would be better, then they can help you with any problems when I'm not here.'

An unexpected cramp cut through her chest. 'Yes, I figured that might be coming. Lizzie will miss you.'

Actually, her mother might too, surprisingly.

'I'll miss her too. But I won't be so far away this time.'

Rhiannon felt the awkwardness returning when the conversation came to a halt. 'Well, I'll leave you to it. I'm just going to take a walk with Winston to clear my head before I go for Lizzie.'

She made a half turn before he stepped forward. 'Or you could give me a hand. That would be helpful.'

Turning back, she watched him make the two long strides it took to get to her, a flutter building in her stomach as he set the pitchfork against the wall and reached for a bottle of water resting between the bars.

'All that heavy straw-shaking getting to you?'

'It's taking more bales than I thought it would, but then making a bed for a pony is hardly an everyday occurrence for me.' He unscrewed the lid of the bottle and tilted it to take a long mouthful of water—right in front of her.

So that she really had no choice but to watch his throat convulse as he swallowed, or to notice how the moisture still rested on his bottom lip afterwards. It brought the term 'water torture' to a whole new level.

'You should have let Lizzie do it; she needs to realize that the pony is her responsibility.'

When he didn't reply, her gaze rose, until she was looking into the darkening blue of his eyes. He'd witnessed her study of him, hadn't he? He knew how aware of him she was, didn't he?

Heat rose on her cheeks. Damn.

'You're not the only one whose work was making them cross-eyed.'

Maybe because he was restless too? For the first time Rhiannon wondered if he was missing his life in Dublin. She knew he had a hugely successful business but she didn't know anything about his private life beyond the odd picture she'd seen of him in glossy mags at big social events with various stunning women at his side. But she was curious now.

Was he in a relationship of some kind? Was he between relationships? Did he just have casual affairs when the need was there? Not that his private affairs had anything to do with her, but she was *definitely* curious. After all, if he ever met someone he got serious with, then that woman would be a part of her daughter's life, wouldn't she?

Somehow that idea didn't sit well with Rhiannon.

Kane set the bottle back down. 'Come on; many hands make light work and all that.'

Without hesitation, he reached out and gently grasped her elbow, coaxing her further into the stable. 'You can shake straw over there and I'll shake straw over here and we'll meet in the middle.'

There was a metaphor in there somewhere.

Rhiannon gently extricated her elbow, looking around the floor for sections of straw to shake out. She could manage to spend a little time in his company one on one doing something simple. *Yes, she could*.

She heard rustling from Kane's side of the stable and, glancing over, saw that he had already gone back to work. He obviously hadn't an issue with her being there, and if he could make the effort then so could she.

So she rolled up the sleeves of her coat a little and bent down to lift a section of straw. 'I'll need to keep an eye on the time for Lizzie.'

'All right, I'll remind you. This shouldn't take long with both of us at it anyway.'

The sound of combined rustling filled the silence for a while as the depth of straw increased on the floor, each of them working from edge to edge on their side of the stable. But as they gradually worked their way closer together Rhiannon became increasing edgy, and the need for some inane chatter to fill the silence became too hard to ignore.

'You must be missing your life in Dublin by now.'

Oh, great. She could have raised a dozen topics, including the weather, but she had to go for one that demonstrated her curiosity. She was a genius.

'Parts of it. But the countryside isn't as boring as I remember it being.'

'That's right; your parents have a place in the country, don't they?' She'd forgotten that. Well, that explained why he'd made an effort with his country clothes, then. He already knew what he was supposed to wear—it was Rhiannon who was still trying to fit in. Just like always.

'Yep, that they do, not that I visit it as often these days, but it was a great place to grow up. Lizzie will love being here.'

And back on to the safe topic of Lizzie again. It suddenly occurred to Rhiannon that maybe she wasn't the only one falling back behind that particular shield.

Rustling filled the silence for a while again. 'I suppose it makes more sense living in the city when you have a hugely successful company to run, though.'

There was an amused edge to his voice. 'Yes, but that's just basic logistics. A company needs staff and there are more people in the city. When it comes to development of the games and new software, that can pretty much be done anywhere.'

Which was why he had been able to stay for so long, right? But that didn't mean his entire life centred on his work—there had to be other things to miss.

'More of a social life in the city, though.'

'Yes, there is. Why, are you missing the bright lights already?'

A glance across at him as he stood tall, shaking straw out in front of him, revealed a teasing light dancing in his eyes and Rhiannon rose to the bait, rolling her eyes. 'Oh, dreadfully. All that clubbing I normally do and the social whirl from one party to the next. You know how it is for we single mothers.'

The minute the last words had left her mouth her gaze locked with his again. Normally, that was exactly the opening he needed to make a caustic comment about how he wouldn't know anything about the life of a parent thanks to her. But instead he smiled wryly.

'Yes, it's exactly the same when you run a large company where hundreds of people rely on you.'

They both reached down for sections of straw while Rhiannon's loose tongue made the comment, 'Well, judging from the number of pictures of you at parties with various women over the years, you've managed to get out and about all right.'

From the corner of her eye she noticed him stop shaking out his section of straw. And she grimaced inwardly, all too aware that she'd just told him he hadn't been invisible to her over the years. It made it sound as if she'd been interested. When at the time she hadn't, not really. It had just been hard to miss all of the pictures was all…

But after a tense moment he started moving again. And she breathed out in relief.

They continued working until they were closer together in the centre of the stable. And, try as she might to concentrate on what she was doing, Rhiannon was only too aware of his every move, of how, even with a task so simple, he had a strength to him that was very palpably male. Just once she would like to spend time with him around and *not* be so aware of that.

She felt the need for chatter again, maybe on a safer topic this time. But before she could raise a topic his deep voice questioned, 'Do you think there's enough in here yet?'

Maybe she wasn't the only one who felt a need to fill the silence, then. She smiled at the thought of Kane Healey ever needing to make small talk, her eyes taking in the depth of the straw so that she could answer him. 'I think that pony is moving into the Ritz Carlton of stables, so yes. And anyway, why are you asking me? You're the one that grew up in the country— ponies were hardly a big part of my life, growing up.'

When she glanced up at him he smiled a slow, dangerous smile. 'Well, my brother and I did have a way of helping our sister check it was deep enough. It always worked for us back then.'

'Okay.' She felt a tingle run up her spine as the smile did things to her heart rate it really had no business doing. So she studied the straw instead and nodded. 'We'll use that method to check it, then.'

'We-ll, if you're sure.'

When she looked back at him there was something about the glint in his eyes that made her wary. 'What exactly *did* you do?'

He pursed his lips together in a way that suggested he was holding back another smile, then stepped towards her with a determined expression on his face. 'We rolled her in it and if she hit the concrete then we knew it needed more.'

Rhiannon gasped. He couldn't seriously—

She held up the armful of straw she still had in warning. 'You wouldn't dare.'

He hesitated very briefly, the glint in his eyes increasing. 'Is that a challenge?'

Automatically spreading her legs a little wider, she bent her knees and faked a dart towards the door, smiling when he went the same way. 'It's a warning.'

She lifted the straw higher.

'Now, Mac—' he tilted his head slightly and looked at her with an amused expression, his legs wider, knees bent in preparation '—I really don't think you want to do that.'

Actually, up until a second ago, she wouldn't have even considered it. But now that he'd warned her not to, a mischievous imp inside her was demanding she did. This was exactly the kind of dumb situation they would have got into back in the day. It was a reminder of lighter, less troublesome, happier times.

And it was maybe exactly what she needed to break through the tension.

So her eyebrows quirked at him. 'Do what?'

His forehead creased into a brief frown, as if he was confused by her reaction. And then, oh, so slowly, another smile started at the corners of his mouth while his voice rumbled out from his chest, low and deep.

'Put the straw down.'

'No-o.' Her mouth formed a circle on the 'o' as she swayed her weight from one leg to the other. 'Because I am *not* being used as a depth test.'

Kane took a deep breath and stood a little more upright, his lashes flickering down against his skin as he nodded. 'Well, I was teasing before.'

Rhiannon relaxed a little, her arms lowering. She'd known that after all, but it had still felt good to have a moment of fun. She'd forgotten what it had been like when they'd done stuff like this. 'Good.'

He nodded again, pursed his lips together again. 'I was— until you just did that.'

She squeaked in surprise as he lunged forward and swept her off her feet, the straw in her arms flying up in the air between them. Her empty arms then sought something to hold on to, her hands grasping hold of his shirt as he swung her backwards and forwards a couple of times.

'One—two—'

Rhiannon laughed uncontrollably, her hands moving up around his neck to hold on tighter. 'Stop it! I swear, Kane, if I go down, you're going with me!'

'You started this.'

'I did not.'

'Consider it an initiation to country life.'

With that, he swung her again and let go. But Rhiannon held on, so that when she fell her weight drew his upper body down with her. Then his feet slipped on the loose straw, dropping him on to his knees. Still laughing, Rhiannon moved quickly, loosening her arms from his neck to grab handfuls of straw and dump them on top of his head.

A battle commenced, with much scrambling and throwing of straw, but ultimately Rhiannon knew it was a battle she couldn't win and after Kane had used his size to his advantage and rolled her back and forth on the straw until she was spluttering, he let go and propped an elbow to lean his head on his hand and look down on her.

'I'd say it's deep enough myself.'

Rhiannon giggled breathlessly, revelling in the fact that she felt lighter than she had in years. And because of Kane, of all people. 'How often did you do this to your poor sister?'

'A lot over the years.' He reached over and pulled a long strand of straw out of her hair. 'It got to be a regular game of cat and mouse.'

'I bet you were a brat.'

'I kinda was.' He smiled down at her. 'I'm just a more grown up version now.'

Rhiannon smiled back. 'Yes, that you are.'

She watched as he focused on her hair, reaching out to remove another strand and toss it to the side. Then he looked into her eyes and in a moment the atmosphere changed, her heart immediately thundering in her chest in response.

He studied her for several long moments, his voice lower when he spoke again. 'This is more like how we used to be, isn't it?'

'Yes, it is.' Her voice was husky in reply, the lightness she'd been feeling replaced with the ache she normally felt when he showed any sign of softness towards her.

He nodded, studied her eyes again and then looked back at her hair, his fingers reaching for a strand close to her face. But this time, when he tossed the strand to the side, those same fingers came back to brush her hair from her neck, stroking briefly against her skin as she swallowed hard.

'Back in the days when you used to like me better.'

Rhiannon couldn't take it if they ended up in yet another debate, so she allowed the truth to slip free. 'I don't hate you so much any more.'

His fingers reached into the neck of her jacket to retrieve more straw, while his dark brows quirked. 'And what exactly did I do to deserve that when you've spent years hating me?'

Her breath hitched as he retrieved a strand of straw from the V of her sweater, the backs of his fingers brushing briefly against the top of her breast. 'I've watched you with Lizzie. And you couldn't be the way you are with her if you were as bad as I convinced myself you were.'

It was only half of the truth, but it was enough to bring his gaze back to lock with hers. And she held her breath as he studied her, her eyes wide as she tried to silently convey her sincerity to him.

When the backs of his fingers brushed gently along her jaw she breathed out, her eyes fluttering shut for a second as a wave of sensation consumed her. She should get up, move away—*far away*—because there was no point in succumbing to just the physical. Not again.

His hand turned, the tips of his fingers moving up along her cheek, across her forehead, where he smoothed out the frown that had formed before tracing the arch of each of her eyebrows in turn.

And, even though she was lying down, Rhiannon had the sensation that she was free falling into the unknown.

But it wasn't the unknown, was it? She knew every single step of this path, as did her body. The body that was awakening to a cornucopia of remembered sensation; her breasts feeling taut and confined, her stomach muscles tensing, an inner trembling forming low in her abdomen and spreading up and out. Because she'd never forgotten what he could do to her with his touch, with his hands and his mouth.

She sighed against the back of his hand when his fingertips traced her lower lip. 'This is a bad idea.'

'I know.'

His voice was so thick and husky that she opened her eyes to confirm what she could hear, her chest tight at the sight of his darkening eyes. She knew that look too.

'Because there's no point in letting this happen again.'

'No, there's not.' His thumb followed his fingertip along her lower lip, then back across her upper lip.

'The only thing we have in common now is our child.'

His eyelids seemed to grow heavier on her use of the word 'our', his head lowering towards hers as he mumbled back, 'Not the only thing, Mac. There's still this.'

The first touch of his mouth was heartbreakingly soft, almost reverent, as if he knew that anything more would have been too much too soon. But Rhiannon moaned low in her throat in protest at her need for more. In an automatic movement born of familiarity, her hand rose, smoothing her fingers into the hair at the back of his head.

Just like she remembered it—a slight coarseness to the touch that made it so very male and yet soft enough to add to the sensuality as her fingers moved.

He traced his mouth across hers from one edge to the other, slow, so slow, then he leaned his head a little closer to make the kiss firmer, deeper. While Rhiannon met each touch and mirrored it, her head spinning.

The fingers that had traced her features turned over, brushed over her cheek, turned again, trailed softly over her jaw and along the arch of her neck to rest on the beating pulse below her ear.

Her fingers tangled further into his hair, began a soft kneading at the back of his head that immediately relaxed his shoulders, and he sank his upper body tighter to hers. And somewhere in her mind she realized that she still knew what felt good for him every bit as much as he was showing her he still knew what felt good to her—because they had history.

But not a future.

She forced her hand out of his hair and went still. And Kane felt it the moment she did because he removed his mouth from hers and leaned back, looking down into her eyes with a silent intensity that tested her resolve to its limits. It would just be so very easy to give in to the temptation of him.

But she couldn't. Not again. Because unbridled passion may have been enough for a brief relationship when she was young and free, but it wasn't enough for her now.

'I should go get Lizzie from school.'

Kane nodded, leaning back to allow her to scramble to her feet before he pushed off his elbow and stood up, raising his hands to brush the straw off his clothes. 'You should get changed first.'

'Yes, I know.' She stepped through the straw and headed out of the stable, not looking back. Because she really needed to stop looking back, didn't she?

CHAPTER TEN

KANE had no idea why he'd let himself kiss her. Up until the very second he had, he most certainly hadn't intended to. And he wasn't best pleased with himself for it either.

They were too tangled up in the past—that was all it was. It was an echo of the way they had used to be and he'd succumbed to that, when really, as a fully grown male, he should have had more self-control.

That was just the thing, though, wasn't it? Ever since he'd walked into the house that first night, his control over things seemed to have been taken from him—piece by piece. It was no wonder he was having difficulty with it.

Being on such shaky ground might have explained why he'd told her the truth about his disappearance all those years ago. *Every action has a reaction.* That was what she'd said. Maybe that was part of the reason he'd told her too. Because she was right about that, wasn't she? If he hadn't got sick when he had, left when he had—

But he'd been twenty-one, for crying out loud! He'd thought he was invincible. Finding out he wasn't had been a lot to take in. And that was putting it mildly.

Actually, all in all, he'd felt he'd coped with it well, dealt with it, put it to the back of his mind and got on with his life.

Until he'd watched Mattie wage the same kind of war and lose…

And that loss had made him re-evaluate just what he had done with his life so far—a natural reaction, he supposed, when he was hit with a case of guilt over why he was still here and Mattie wasn't.

The sight of Lizzie trying to wrestle a stuffed monkey from the jaws of her new 'puppy' dragged a smile on to his mouth. Just watching her lifted his spirits in a way he couldn't remember them ever lifting before. And every day he spent with her—even if they talked complete nonsense or did nothing particularly exciting—had him more in love with her than he'd been the day before. She was a miracle after all, wasn't she? The child he'd resigned himself to never having.

And he knew he had Rhiannon to thank for that miracle and its associated joy. They had made this child together. And that bound him to Rhiannon for the rest of his life in a way that went beyond just the physical. The same physical he had given in to so damn quickly again after ten minutes rolling around in some straw.

She'd always had that effect on him. From the first day she'd flashed a smile at him across the counter of the coffee shop facing Trinity. A smile, a sparkle in her eyes, a mild flirtation that he'd soon looked forward to every day. That was all it had taken for him to be drawn in until he was almost addicted to her.

But he'd been a twenty-one-year-old typically hormone-driven male. He hadn't thought about things like the future or how miscommunication would have a long-term effect on both of them and the child they made. Life had been an adventure, a game, with days to be filled with nothing more complicated than fun and laughter.

It had taken the chance discovery of a lump for him to re-evaluate everything.

He leaned back, resting his weight on his elbows as he stretched his legs out, crossing them at the ankles. Then he tilted his head back, eyes closing, as he allowed the imagined warmth of the late January sun to put a red glow on the backs of his eyelids while he took a deep breath of the crisp air.

Knowing that Lizzie was a product of his time with Rhiannon was constantly pushing more and more of the memories into his mind from an earlier trouble-free time in his life. But there hadn't been any point in remembering, had there? That time had been gone. Breaking up with Rhiannon had been on a long 'to-do' list that he'd made to break contact with a world where people didn't have to face up to their own mortality.

But again he wondered: if he hadn't been sick, if he hadn't broken up with her—if he'd waited to see where that first flush of purely sexual attraction had taken them in the long term…

Kane hated 'ifs'. And now he had dozens of the damn things. In business he always researched variables—but in his personal life? Well, not so much. Because in his personal life he made quite sure there were no variables to begin with. He was always careful not to get involved with the kind of women who wanted long term—things like marriage and two-point-four of the kids he couldn't give them without the help of the medical profession.

But to add to all the variables he *now* had, he had to add another; whatever physical attraction there had been between Rhiannon and him before—was still there.

The kiss in the straw had proved that.

It had probably been creeping up on him a little more with each day he spent near her. And when he had witnessed that look of distress on her face after he'd told her the truth, he'd wanted to kiss the pity out of her eyes, to prove to her that he was still very much alive, still very much one hundred per cent male even if he couldn't ever make another Lizzie with her.

Which begged the question of whether that could be the

reason he'd kissed her this last time? Was there a part of him that felt it had to prove himself to her?

Opening his eyes, he dropped his chin, automatically turning his head towards the French windows at the back of the house, beyond which Rhiannon had been spending more and more of her time since the day in the stable. Most likely hiding—well, that was what he'd guessed she was doing—at first.

His gaze strayed back to Lizzie; her laughter echoed off the walls of the house, and he smiled again. But after a while he ended up looking back towards the windows, a breeze lifting the end of the long curtains out through a small gap that called to him.

Come on in—you know you want to.

He pursed his mouth in thought, because he *was* tempted. He wasn't so sure any more that Rhiannon was hiding, not judging by the dark shadows in her eyes at dinner the last couple of nights. And if there was a problem, then he needed to know about it. Forewarned was forearmed…

'Kane!' Lizzie stopped tugging the stuffed monkey, waiting until Kane looked at her before she grinned and asked, 'Can we take Winston up by the lake like we did yesterday? He loved it.'

'All right.' He uncrossed his ankles and pushed up on to his feet, lifting the jacket he had been sitting on and shaking it while his eyes strayed yet again to the open windows. 'Give me a minute and we'll see if your mum wants to come too. She might need some fresh air.'

'Okay.'

Rhiannon didn't hear him come in. He knew that the minute he stepped past the curtain and saw her resting her face in her hands. As if somehow sensing his presence, she glanced up, her soft brown eyes widening a little in surprise while she pushed long tendrils of auburn hair that had escaped her pony-tail off her flushed cheeks.

'Hello.' The greeting was soft, maybe a little cautious, and

Kane felt a momentary longing for the brief ease there had been between them before he'd kissed her. 'It can't be time for lunch already.'

He watched as she glanced at her watch, her finely arched brows then rising in question. 'Is something wrong?'

'Nope, we're fine. Lizzie wanted to know if you fancied going for a walk, so I said I'd ask.' He kept studying her, the changes in the tones of colour in her eyes as she thought, the way she moved her head, how her sweater rose and fell as she breathed.

Then her eyes softened, a smile curling her lips upwards. 'I could certainly do with a break.'

Kane smiled back at her, glanced away when it felt awkward, even momentarily considered just staying in the open doorway where he could make a swift withdrawal to the safety of Lizzie. But instead he found himself drawn into the room and perching on the edge of the huge old leather-topped desk Mattie had once sat behind when they'd talked business and life in general.

This had been the room where they could talk with ease and without boundaries—about the kinds of things Kane could never seem to talk to other people about—like being scared, which wasn't something any man ever liked to confess to…

He cleared his throat, then, with a quick glance down at the open books, paperwork and bills scattered over the surface of the desk, he risked looking back at Rhiannon's face. And, unbidden, his earlier thoughts about Lizzie being the child they had made together slammed into the front of his skull, vividly this time, with Technicolor detailed memories of 'how' it had happened.

Yep, and there it was again. That immediate physical awareness of her—even stronger now with the additional Technicolor details and the memory of their last kiss. Admittedly, Rhiannon may have been pretty when he had known her at eighteen, but she was an entirely different woman at twenty-nine. She'd blossomed into adult womanhood, with more lush curves than she'd

had when he'd known her so intimately, curves he'd been all
too aware of when he'd been lying with her on a bed of straw.

That physical awareness had probably been there from the
first night in the kitchen. And, before they had begun to communicate better, he'd been mad as hell at her for that, hadn't he?
He hadn't wanted it to be there, hadn't sought it out. It was another example of the lack of control he seemed to have when she
was around. And now that he'd given in to it once already…?

Well, now a part of him couldn't help but wonder what she'd
do if he pursued it…

'You're still working on the house accounts?'

A shadow of doubt crossed her eyes, then she dismissed it
with a sigh. And Kane knew how she felt. It wasn't as if either
of them were the open book type. But this whole 'getting along
for Lizzie's sake' had to be a two-way street, didn't it? One little
kiss couldn't get in the way. And he was fully prepared to use
that line of reasoning if he had to, especially having told her
more than he ever intended to about himself already.

But, before he could decide what route to take, she took a
breath, her gaze dropping to where her fingers were shuffling
papers back and forth for no apparent reason. 'It's a lot to take
in. I mean, I've worked on accounts before but these…'

He watched as she shook her head, loose strands of hair
trailing over her shoulders. 'It's a large place.'

'Yes and a huge responsibility.'

'Mattie must have thought you were up to it.'

Rhiannon surprised him by laughing softly as she leaned back
in the large chair. 'Well, he may possibly have got that one wrong.'

The words surprised him again. From what he'd understood
over the years, Rhiannon had been the only one who had understood Mattie's passion for Brookfield. It wasn't as if huge
country estates were all that common any more and it took a
particular personality to enjoy the constant upkeep a place like

this would take. It was a lifetime's work. At one time a legacy handed on from generation to generation—almost like a crown from one generation of royalty to another.

And for a long time in Ireland, the people who'd owned a legacy like this one had been universally hated, to the extent of being run off the land before their homes were burned to the ground. But Brookfield had somehow survived all that and was now in the hands of an Irishwoman. It was Rhiannon's legacy to hand on to Lizzie, wasn't it?

Which was another reason for Kane to be involved in any problem there might be, right? It had to do with Lizzie's future—his daughter's future—and *her* legacy. And that made it his business.

A sudden thought brought a frown to his face.

'What?' Rhiannon leaned forward in her chair, resting her elbows on top of the papers.

'I was right, wasn't I? This place can't look after itself without the income from the estate.' He didn't need an answer; he could see it on her face. 'How long did Mattie know about Lizzie?'

Rhiannon blinked in confusion. 'I don't see—'

'How long?' He leaned his upper body a little more in her direction and kept his voice calm. 'I'm not trying to start another argument; I just need to know.'

Recognition of the same words she'd used to coax his biggest secret from him seemed to persuade her to volunteer the information.

'I think he probably knew early on. He kept coming into the coffee shop long after you'd gone and it was only then that we really became friends.' She smiled at a memory. 'He brought Lizzie her first teddy bear at the hospital. But he didn't ask me outright until just before I married Stephen.'

Kane nodded again. Yeah, that was what he'd figured.

Rhiannon's eyes narrowed a little. 'Am I missing something?'

'There was always method in Mattie's madness. I should have known there was more to it.' Kane shook his head this time, a wry smile crossing his lips. 'He knew rightly what he was doing.'

'All right—you've lost me.'

He pushed up off the desk, glancing towards the open doors before he smiled and cocked his head in their direction. 'Come for a walk and I'll maybe tell you what I think.'

He hit her with a raised brows silent challenge, and smiled more when she rolled her eyes and chuckled. All right, so maybe getting along better with Rhiannon wasn't that bad a thing. And he felt a little more in control again, which felt good, if a little ironic considering he'd just realized that they'd both been manipulated to where they were.

'All right then.' She pushed back from the desk, still smiling as she walked past him. 'You've got me. I'll grab a coat. I'm a sucker for a mystery.'

'Well, this one's not my doing.' He stood up, teasing her in a low voice, 'You've already wheedled out all my darkest secrets.'

She turned around and walked backwards for a few steps, her head tilting flirtatiously. 'I doubt very much that I know them all.'

Kane studied her for a long moment. 'You know enough.'

'Yes.' The word was spoken softly, with a matching small smile and a light in her eyes that he couldn't quite read from across the room. 'Enough to know what I need to know, I guess.'

He stood in the empty room long after she'd left, not waiting for her but just *thinking*. What *was it* with him and this woman?

They were halfway around the lake, their exhaled breath forming puffs of steam in the cold air before Rhiannon couldn't take any more of the suspense.

Not that walking side by side talking about nothing more difficult than Lizzie's antics with Winston and pointing out wildlife as it appeared wasn't a moment of acquiescence that she subliminally recognized as a rare experience of camaraderie. But she was still curious as all hell about what he'd figured out in the library.

Just in case it was something that would lead them to awkwardness or harsh words again, she savoured the moment, tilting her head back to watch the breeze push the clouds by overhead before she closed her eyes and filled her lungs with a deep breath of cool winter air. And she smiled contentedly.

'You really do love it here, don't you?' Kane's deep voice sounded close by her shoulder.

When she opened her eyes and lifted her gaze to his, she smiled a smaller smile, suddenly feeling shy again, which wasn't really all that surprising, considering the last time she'd been 'alone' with him. And, even with Lizzie disappearing and reappearing out of the trees from time to time, they *were* still alone, weren't they?

The thought made her pulse skip. 'Yep.'

He nodded and stopped at the edge of the water, his gaze searching the ground while he spoke. 'Did you know Mattie planned on leaving you this place?'

'No.' She frowned as he bent over and selected a few round, flat stones, tossing them into the palm of his other hand. Surely he didn't think she'd done something to influence Mattie's decision? They'd been friends, better than friends—more like brother and sister. Mattie had been her family when she didn't have one any more. When her own family had turned her away—the 'good child' who had made a horrible mistake proving too difficult for them to even look at…

'I think he knew he was leaving it to you for a long time. In fact—' inhaling, he stood up again, glancing briefly at her before he started sorting through the stones in his hand '—I'm pretty sure he knew when he offered to sell me the estate.'

Rhiannon stepped closer, watching as he selected one of the

stones and stepped back on to one foot, swinging his arm out in an arc to throw the stone so that it skipped over the water's surface—once, twice, three times before it sank.

And he grinned across at her like a small boy. 'I was hoping I hadn't forgotten how to do that.'

Her heart caught.

'You have no idea how much you remind me of Lizzie when you smile like that.' Her eyes widened in surprise at the confession. They just seemed to constantly roll off the end of her tongue these days, didn't they?

But Kane merely continued grinning. 'Yeah.' He leaned back to toss another stone over the water. 'She's good-looking too.'

Rhiannon shook her head. Who *was* this man? Every day she was more and more enraptured by the different facets of his personality. And every day he would do or say something that knocked her off balance. She should have been mad about that, especially after the kiss that had still lingered on her lips hours after the event. But it was difficult to stay mad when he was like this—so charming, so good-looking, so damn irresistible.

'Well, thankfully she has me to keep her ego from growing to continental proportions.' She refocused on the topic of their conversation. 'What makes you so sure Mattie had planned that far ahead?'

Kane tossed the stones he had left in his hand up and down a couple of times, taking a breath of crisp air before he shrugged the shoulders beneath his heavy down-lined jacket. 'I think he knew for a long time that he was fighting a battle he'd lose. He fought for a lot longer than I had to with mine and I think he was resigned to just buying as much time as he could. But it gave him time to think about things and to make plans. It's the kind of guy he was. He thought about the people he cared about, and what would happen to them when he wasn't here any more.'

Rhiannon immediately wondered if Kane had had to make

those kinds of plans once—had thought about not being here any more—about his own death. How must that have felt at so young an age to someone so very alive?

And who had he talked to? For a man like him to confess any kind of weakness would have cost dearly, wouldn't it? When going away and facing his illness, fighting it, coming out the other side, had taken more bravery than she could even begin to respect him enough for having.

Her heart twisted painfully at another thought. How would she have felt if something had happened to him? No one would probably have thought she should know, except maybe Mattie. Yes, Mattie would have made sure she didn't read it in a paper somewhere. But it would have hurt. She knew that. It would have hurt so very much, maybe even worse than losing Mattie had.

But it wouldn't have hurt anywhere near as much as it would if anything happened to Kane now...

He glanced at her from the corner of his eye, a thoughtful expression on his ruggedly handsome face. 'Do you know how to skim stones?'

'What?' She shook her head, laughing a little to cover the dark thoughts that still hovered in her mind—troubled, confused thoughts that forced her to concentrate twice as hard to keep up with their conversation without giving anything away.

He leaned down and selected a larger handful of stones. 'They need to be fairly round, and as flat as possible or they don't bounce.'

'You're insane. I don't suppose you happen to know where Kane Healey went to? Big guy, pretty grumpy most of the time, prone to starting a topic of conversation and then gets easily sidetracked by children's games...'

She watched in amused amazement as he stepped closer, reaching out to tug at her elbow with his empty hand so that she was forced to pull her hand out of her pocket while he beckoned with his fingers.

'Give me your hand.'

'I can't do what you just did.'

'Don't be a girl.'

Even while his warm fingers curled beneath her hand so he could place a stone in her palm, she was looking up at his profile with raised eyebrows.

And he smiled again in response, his cheeks creasing into a hint of dimples as he glanced at her face and then down at her hand. 'All right then, try being *less* of a girl.'

The mischievous imp reappeared on her shoulder and forced her to bat her eyelashes frantically at him.

Still smiling, he moved round behind her, concentrating his focus on her hand as he moved her fingers into position. 'Curl your forefinger around the top, thumb round the bottom and then, when you throw, you flick your wrist back and, as you flick forwards, you let go. Try to keep it as flat as you can along the surface of the water and it'll skip.'

His hand still supporting hers, his gaze rose, and Rhiannon had to lean her head back further to lock eyes with him. It was disconcerting as all hell having him this close again, it really was. How was a girl supposed to do anything but stare?

The breeze caught his hair and ruffled it, his thick lashes brushed against the faint tinge of red the chilled air had created on his cheeks and his bluer than blue eyes warmed her as he continued softly smiling. And, just as it had done since the first day she had met him, Rhiannon's heart thundered against her breast and her nerve-endings tingled from head to toe in response. She even had to consciously stop herself from turning around and stepping in against him, tilting her head back in invitation, to…

She swallowed hard. 'All right, but just so you know, it'll

sink like…' she grinned as the words formed in her head '…well, it'll sink like a stone, *obviously*. But it'll sink. Trust me.'

'We'll practise a couple of times.' He blinked down at her, then lifted his gaze and looked out over the greyish blue of the water. 'And once you have it mastered, you can come down here and skim stones with Lizzie when I'm not here.'

Rhiannon swiftly turned her face away, her heart still thudding hard, but now accompanied by a dull ache in the pit of her stomach. She knew he would leave, had known all along—this time round. And at least this time when he left they'd be on friendly enough terms to be able to arrange visits for Lizzie and times when he could come back down to Brookfield. And she would be able to hold a conversation with him. It was all good, right?

Hand still on hers, he guided her arm out in an arc to her side. 'Put your weight back on to one foot and then, as you swing your arm, move your weight on to your front foot before you let go of the stone.'

She let him guide her movements in a couple of practice sways, his large body cushioning hers, aware that the simple act of throwing a stone across the water had somehow morphed into a seductive dance movement.

'Now have a go.' He stepped back before she threw and watched in silence as the stone sank without as much as a hint of a bounce.

With a brief glance over her shoulder, she blew her cheeks out and announced smugly, 'I told you so.'

With a chuckle and a shake of his head, he stepped round her again, lifting her hand to tip the remainder of the stones into her palm. 'Keep practising; you'll get it.'

Gathering more stones from the ground while she watched, he then stood beside her and tossed another one on to the water—skip, skip, sink.

'So, anyway…' he watched her make another failed attempt at skimming a stone '…I think Mattie knew when he sold me the estate that one day you would own the house. It was his way of forcing us into a locked room so we'd have to talk.'

Rhiannon stopped mid-swing. *'What?'*

'Yep.' His voice stayed calm as he swung again—skip, skip, skip, sink. 'He knew the estate and the house needed each other to survive, and he made quite sure I couldn't sell one without the other. I doubt he was even as badly off financially as he claimed to be. We were manipulated into dealing with all of this.'

Rhiannon couldn't believe what she was hearing, but in a heartbeat it suddenly made absolute sense. 'Why, that wily—'

'Exactly.' Kane stunned her by continuing to smile as he tossed another stone—skip, skip, skip, sink. 'He knew how stubborn we both were. And he knew we'd both built a firm set of misconceptions about each other—'

'So he decided to try and find a way to *fix it*?'

He stood still, his focus on the horizon as he nodded. 'Yes, I think so. I've only just figured it out now, but I'm pretty sure that's what he did. I remember he said a lot of things about the house and the estate having to work together, about partnerships and how a history like that can tie people together, grounding them. And I listened, but I don't think I really understood what he was saying, until now.'

Mesmerized by the familiar deep rumble of his voice, laced as it was in that moment with a warm edge of nostalgia, it took a moment for her to realize that he was looking at her again. When she did, her gaze rose slowly, locking with his as she felt a sense of inevitability sweeping over her.

'You see this place as your legacy for Lizzie, don't you—something that'll be here long after you're gone?'

Rhiannon nodded silently, deeply touched in a way she couldn't even begin to quantify.

'Well, I want my part of her legacy to be the estate. The way it should be—the two working together to survive in the future. Half of it yours to pass on and half of it mine.'

'You don't have to do that.' Somehow she managed to choke the words out through her thickening throat.

He shook his head, his gaze steady and determined. 'Yes, I do. And I want to.'

Rhiannon remained frozen to the same spot as he stepped closer, his voice huskier, filled with emotion as he told her in the same steady, determined tone, with his gaze locked on hers, 'I love her, Mac, I do. Whether it's too soon to feel something that strong or not, it's there. My world now revolves around her.'

Just as she had felt the very moment she had first held her baby in her arms. 'I know.'

'So it's what I want to do to provide for her future, and the rest of the stuff in between we can work out between us. I think we can do that now, can't we?'

'Yes.' She nodded to emphasize the word that came out on so low a tone that it was almost a whisper, her eyes filling as she looked at him. Because there was a huge bubble of emotion filling her chest while she did and she just couldn't stop it from spilling over. It had formed the moment he'd said he loved Lizzie. The only child he believed he might ever have.

'I want to tell her now, if that's all right with you. I don't think there's any need to wait any more.'

He nodded, still staring at her with his intense blue-eyed gaze as he moved another step closer, stopping a few inches away from her body.

'Yes, it's time—maybe after dinner? Then she can ask us both any questions she has and we can talk her through it together.'

Together. Rhiannon nodded, still frozen to the spot.

He cleared his throat. 'Do you know what you'll say yet?'

She laughed nervously, lifting a hand to swipe at the lone tear she felt streaking down her cheek. 'I haven't the faintest idea. I'm hoping I'll find the right ones when I sit her down. It's not easy explaining to your own child that you're not infallible when you've allowed them to believe you are.'

Without hesitation a large hand rose to her face, where he spread his fingers, snaking them back into the base of her ponytail while his thumb brushed along the fine line of her jaw until it rested at the edge of her mouth. Then he leaned his face down closer to hers, studying each of her eyes in turn.

'Mac, you've done everything to take care of her every step of the way. And you've done one hell of a job. Whatever you say will be just fine.'

The use of the old endearment hit her again. He'd used it in the stable that day too, hadn't he? How had she missed that? Accompanied by his softly spoken vote of confidence in her when she needed to hear it the most, it was almost too much. And she could feel the wall she'd erected around her heart so many years ago crumbling.

If she could go back in time, she would never have held this man from his child. Why would she? He was amazing. Any child would be lucky to have him as their father. Her own anger, pain, fear, confusion and eventual resentment had held them apart. How could he ever forgive her for that?

As if he could read her thoughts, a small frown appeared between his eyes, the blue deepened, his gaze dropped to her mouth. And, somewhere in the distance, Rhiannon heard stones dropping to the ground.

Then his other hand was on her face, fingers snaking into her hair, thumb moving to rest against her mouth; so that he held her head cradled in his palms with infinite tenderness.

Rhiannon sighed shakily, her eyelids growing heavy.

'Mum?'

Kane stepped back from her as if burned, and they both turned to look at Lizzie's curious expression.

'What are you doing?' She smiled impishly—she had a fairly vivid idea already of what they were doing.

'I'm teaching your mum to skim stones and she was having a crisis of confidence because she can't do it.' Kane cleared his throat. 'You want to learn?'

'*Oooh*, yes, I do!'

He retrieved the stones from the ground before she got there, glancing over her head at Rhiannon as he started to repeat the instructions.

And Rhiannon stared back at him, desperate to know if he regretted almost kissing her again—if it had merely been a reflection of the intense emotions they both felt talking about their daughter and her future, or if it had been because he knew how much her feelings for him had changed.

Instead she watched as Lizzie made her first attempt at skimming the stone, her small arm swinging back, the stone flying through the air—skip, sink.

First time.

CHAPTER ELEVEN

THE decision to tell Lizzie was taken out of their hands by an unexpected arrival when they returned to the house.

Rhiannon had never set eyes on her before, but the warmly smiling woman soon apologized for 'popping by' unannounced and introduced herself as the Chairperson of the annual Hunt Ball, which was normally held before Christmas at Brookfield, apparently. And over a pot of tea at the kitchen table she explained how they had postponed the Ball out of respect for Mattie's passing. Then she announced that they'd like to reschedule, with Rhiannon's permission, of course. At Brookfield, if it was all right with her.

In the space of an hour Rhiannon found herself agreeing to the event being held there for Valentine's Day, as it was a century-old tradition, and with Kane offering to step in and sponsor it, thankfully, while Lizzie bounced up and down at the prospect of a large party and a new dress to go with it, naturally.

Rhiannon was left feeling distinctly railroaded.

But it was outside on the gravel, as they all saw the nice lady to her car, that the damage was done.

'Thank you so much, dear. I know the committee will be over the moon with the news.' She beamed at Rhiannon, looked at Kane with an admiring glance and then patted Lizzie's head.

'And *you* are an absolute darling. I can't wait to see you in your new dress.'

'Me either!' Lizzie grinned up at her.

'She really is just beautiful.' The woman's eyes skimmed up to Kane's face again. 'And you look just like your daddy too, don't you?'

Rhiannon gasped. *Oh, no.* She *had not* just said that!

Lizzie looked over her shoulder and up at Kane, who stared down at her with the same stunned expression Rhiannon knew had to be written all over her own face.

The cheery voice continued. 'Oh, yes, she really is the image of you, there's no denying it. She has your eyes and your hair colour, doesn't she?'

Kane swallowed hard, his helpless gaze flickering to Rhiannon's before they both watched Lizzie turn round and start to slowly work it out.

'Well, I'll be in touch soon.' She pulled open her car door and ran the window down to wave. 'Lovely family. Super to meet you at last. Cheerio!'

Lizzie stood with her head tilted to one side, a frown creasing her forehead as she continued to study Kane's face. And it was only the edge to Kane's voice that drew Rhiannon out of her horrified silence.

'We need to go inside.'

'Yes, we do.' She stepped over to Lizzie and smoothed a hand over her hair. 'Come on, baby. We'll all go into the sitting room and we can have a talk.'

Lizzie silently studied Kane as she walked past him, while her mother grasped her father's hand, tangling their fingers together and squeezing.

He looked down at her as she whispered, 'I'm so sorry. It shouldn't have happened like this.'

His longer fingers wrapped tighter around hers. 'It's not your fault. We'll talk to her together, okay?'

Rhiannon nodded. Because there really wasn't much else to say, was there?

In the sitting room Kane released her hand and walked over to Lizzie, setting his large hand on her shoulder to guide her around the sofa, where he sat down and obviously assumed she'd sit with him.

But, before Rhiannon's wide eyes, she stood in front of Kane and reached her small hands up to frame his face, leaning in closer to stare at his eyes close up. She tilted her head, one chocolate-brown braid swinging over her shoulder.

'You have blue eyes, like me.'

Rhiannon pursed her lips tightly together, her heart twisting, tears filling her eyes as Kane nodded, his voice husky and filled with immeasurable gentleness.

'Yes, I do.'

Lizzie lifted a hand and caught a lock of his short hair between her fingers, studying it carefully before she looked down at the swinging braid, then back into his eyes. 'And brown hair, like me.'

'Yes.'

Rhiannon stepped closer, her hand smoothing over Lizzie's hair again as she bent down. 'Not quite, baby.'

Two sets of matching blue eyes stared at her. And she had to swallow hard to damp down a wave of emotion before she continued, 'You have blue eyes like *his*. And brown hair like *his*. Because, you see, he really *is* your dad.'

Lizzie's eyes widened before she looked back at Kane's face. *'Really?'*

He nodded again. 'Yes, really.'

The smile took a moment, but when it arrived her whole face seemed to light up from within, as if everything she had ever wanted with all of her young heart had just been set in front of her.

'I'm glad,' she announced with conviction.

Kane swallowed hard, his voice firmer. 'So am I.'

'Where were you?'

The question broke Rhiannon's heart in two. She opened her mouth to say something, but couldn't find the right words, instead listening with silent admiration as Kane answered the question with *exactly* the right words.

'Waiting for you.'

Lizzie threw herself forward, her small arms wrapping around his neck and holding on tight. And Rhiannon watched as Kane's eyes closed and he wrapped his arms around her waist, lifting her up off the ground, his face contorting briefly in what might have looked like agony to someone who didn't know better.

But Rhiannon knew what it was, even before his eyes opened and his gaze followed the path of the fat, heavy tears streaking down her cheeks, forcing her to raise a hand to her mouth to cover a sob.

Why had she ever kept them apart? She knew she would never forgive herself for that. Not after this. Because she'd never have found the perfect words he just had.

Had she ever really known this man? He was so different from the one she had known before and yet in so many ways just the same. She was certainly as attracted to him physically as she had been before, but this new version of him affected her on so many other levels. And the combination of his words by the lake and seeing him with his daughter now that she knew who he was so heart-rending, so very precious to both of them, that Rhiannon couldn't have not loved him for being the father he was to her child.

She pushed herself upright, watching her child as she turned her cheek against her father's chest, nestling in with her eyes closed and a contented expression on her face. Then, just as Rhiannon turned to walk away, she felt her eyes drawn inexorably back to Kane's face.

He smiled up at her, his heart in his eyes. And that simple smile shattered her completely, tearing her heart from her chest and fading the rest of the world away so that the only thing she could see for a second was him. But she simply nodded, managed an answering smile and mouthed a, 'Thank you.'

It wasn't anywhere near enough, but she meant it, in so many more ways than just 'thank you for being everything Lizzie deserves'.

Fearful that anything more than that would show in her eyes, she stepped back, then turned and left the room, the tears flowing freely down her cheeks as she left them behind. Because what was happening in that room was nothing to do with her, was it? For the first time in her young child's life there was something that Rhiannon couldn't share, couldn't be a part of and never would. She couldn't stay there and watch as father and daughter bonded, became irretrievably bound to each other. But not because she was jealous or didn't want the bond to exist—not when they both needed each other as much as they did—but because Rhiannon wanted so badly to be able to share in what they had.

And it broke her heart that they were two halves of a family that just didn't fit together to make a whole. Maybe even to make *her* feel whole in a way she'd never felt before.

They eventually found Rhiannon in the kitchen, after a long time in the sitting room with Lizzie sitting across his lap, her arms around his neck while she brightly informed him how very pleased she was to have a dad of her own before she asked a dozen questions about her new family.

But even though Kane savoured every single second of a

time he knew he would never forget, he felt the lack of Rhiannon's presence in the room, almost as if there was something missing because she wasn't there.

Not that he didn't deeply appreciate the time she'd given them alone, because he did. But somehow, as Lizzie's line of questioning dwindled a little, it felt wrong not to have her mother there too. So he leaned his forehead in against Lizzie's to whisper, 'Let's go find your mum.'

She held on to his hand all the way to the kitchen, only releasing him to bounce up on to the long bench and announce in an excited voice, 'I have grandparents and an uncle and an auntie and cousins and everything!'

Rhiannon smiled at her from the Aga end of the room. 'That's amazing, isn't it?'

It suddenly occurred to Kane that Lizzie was more excited by that than he'd thought she'd be. Didn't Rhiannon have brothers or sisters? He vaguely remembered a brother somewhere. And, as to the grandparents…

'You already have a set of grandparents, don't you?' He moved further into the room, swinging a long leg over the bench opposite Lizzie.

Lizzie shook her head firmly. 'Nope. I had Stephen's mum and dad as kind of almost grandparents for a while, but they weren't really mine. And Mum's parents never knowed me.'

He scowled, his gaze immediately drawn to Rhiannon's face across the room. Why not? Had something happened to them? Surely he'd have heard that from Mattie, if no one else? Not, he guessed, that he'd ever been that open to hearing anything about Rhiannon when he'd shut all thought of her out of his mind and been determined to believe that she'd moved swiftly on from the brief relationship they'd had. And he'd been damn quick to make that assumption, hadn't he?

Maybe it had eased his conscience, because it'd been easier to believe he hadn't thrown away something that might have been important. How in hell would he have known if it was important at twenty-one? He'd been too wrapped up in other things…

Lizzie, as usual, continued to deliver reams of the kind of information it would have taken him weeks to get out of her mother. 'They didn't think Mum should have a baby 'cos she was too young and all. But Mum wanted me more than anything in the whole world so she left home and had me. And we made our own family.'

Rhiannon grimaced before she could hide it and Kane swore inwardly in response. That was what she'd meant when she'd said she knew what it was like to have a father reject her? They had turned her away?

They had turned their own daughter away?

No wonder she'd hated him for not being there. The father of her baby had disappeared off the face of the earth, her parents had disowned her and she didn't have a well-paid job or any kind of financial support. It all added together to form a mental picture that Kane found very difficult to see.

And the huge wave of anger that formed inside him must have shown because Rhiannon's soft voice sounded again from across the room, with a tone of reassurance.

'And we did just fine didn't we, baby?'

Lizzie nodded, oblivious to the undercurrents. 'Better now that Kane's here, though.'

Kane smiled at her, then glanced at Rhiannon, who smiled back at him but couldn't seem to look him in the eye. 'Yes, better now.'

He knew she meant better for Lizzie's sake. But he also discovered a part of him hoped she meant it a little from her point of view too. He'd like it if she thought his being there, being a part of their lives, was better for all of them. That was the way it was supposed to be, wasn't it? It was part of a father's remit, after all—to take care of his family.

The thought would have knocked him off his feet if he'd been upright. Instead he tried to complete the missing parts of the puzzle. 'Where did you live?'

Rhiannon didn't look overly surprised by the question. 'A friend of mine from the coffee shop let me rent a room at her place. And I worked full-time until I had Lizzie, and then went part-time until she was older.'

'Auntie Kerri.'

'That's right.' Rhiannon shrugged as if it weren't as big a deal as Kane knew it was. 'When Kerri worked at night in one of the bars near the campus I looked after her kids and she helped with Lizzie when I worked. It worked for both of us; we've been friends ever since.'

Kane frowned harder. She'd made sacrifices to bring his child into the world; had told that child that she'd been wanted more than anything else, had raised her to be bright, happy, well balanced. No small achievement in the world they lived in. While the father who could have provided everything they needed and more had dropped off the planet. Even when he'd been ill, even if he hadn't recovered, he'd still have provided for them both. Didn't she know that?

How could she *not* know that?

Rhiannon smiled again. 'We were fine.'

'What about the course you were doing at night?'

She looked surprised he remembered. Hadn't she got that part yet? They may not have been in love back then, but he remembered *everything*. He made an attempt to silently communicate that to her, almost testing her to see if she could read his thoughts as well as he'd started to read hers.

But, even though she faltered, she shrugged it off again, literally, in a way that was really starting to irritate the hell out of Kane. 'I kept going for as long as I could. When I had Lizzie I quit so I could look after her; young baby, part-time work and course work weren't a good combination. So something had to give.'

'But she finished it in the post when I was bigger. 'Cos school is important and she needed it for her work when I was big enough for school.'

Rhiannon clarified it for him. 'I switched to an Open University course. Took a bit longer but I still finished it. And then I did temp work as a PA, which paid better than the coffee shop career. It was fine.'

Fine. She kept using that word, didn't she? Well, it damn well wasn't fine with him. Fine wasn't anywhere near good enough.

'Motherhood matures you'—she'd thrown something like that at him right at the start of his stay at Brookfield, hadn't she? How much had she been trying to tell him between the lines that he'd missed? What else had he got wrong when he'd simply thought she'd held his child from him out of spite?

It hadn't been spite. He'd dumped her and left; she hadn't known why because he hadn't wanted to tell her—to show anyone for a single second that he was less of a man or might be less of a man by the end of his treatment. So, for all she knew, he didn't give a toss about her. She'd tried to get in contact with him and while he didn't answer her parents had disowned her and she'd been alone. Any wonder she'd believed he didn't give a damn. It had probably felt as if no one had, so she'd just knuckled down and got on with it.

All those years she'd worked hard to provide for Lizzie, just to keep their heads above water—she'd still managed to finish her education so that she could improve her career prospects—until—

'You didn't have to work when you married Stephen.' He clenched his teeth on the words.

It still bugged the hell out of him that that had happened. And knowing what he did now made it worse. Because Stephen hadn't just got to spend time with *his* child; he'd had Rhiannon.

He'd wanted everything of Kane's from their days in grammar school. She must have seemed like the ultimate prize to him and that was why it had been so easy for Kane to believe he'd moved in on her the second he was gone. Lord alone knew he had hung around the coffee shop enough when she'd been there—hell, even when Kane had been dating her. And Kane had had to warn him off often enough…

He'd thought when they got married it was just Stephen finally being a man and accepting his responsibilities. Had that just been another false belief for Kane to ease his conscience?

Whatever way he looked at it, he was finding himself falling desperately short of being much of a guy. And that just didn't sit well with him. Not just in the fatherhood department either. It mattered to him with Mac too.

'No, I still worked, not that Stephen liked it too much. And marrying him was a mistake; it didn't last long. We lived apart for most of it, and when we divorced I rented the house in Dublin from him.'

Kane's hands bunched into fists below the table.

'He wanted me to go to stupid boarding school.' Lizzie rolled her eyes.

'I didn't let that happen, did I?' Rhiannon added, more quietly this time, so that Kane's gaze immediately flew to lock with hers before she blinked and looked away. 'It's all history now.'

He watched as Rhiannon moved across the room to plant a kiss on the top of Lizzie's head. 'And that's probably enough information for one night. There's chicken for dinner.'

'Yay!'

'I'm going to have a bath; I take it I can trust you two to make sure nothing gets burnt to a crisp?' She glanced at him briefly again from the corner of her eye. And that one look told him he'd heard more than she would have ever volunteered. She still felt the need to hide things from him—but why? What else was she holding back?

If she really thought he was done with her, then she had another think coming. He was a member of this family now; the sense of protectiveness that filled him was overwhelming now, though not so much for feeling protective of Lizzie—that was a given—it was the sudden need to extend that protectiveness to Rhiannon that surprised him the most. When exactly *had that* happened?

He'd known all about the early resentment he felt when he'd been so aware of how she moved, how soft her hair looked, how her thoughts would cross over her expressive eyes. He was all too conscious of the physical attraction that flared every time he was near her—because he'd even come dangerously close to kissing her again by the lake before they'd been interrupted, hadn't he?

And he had spent the walk back wondering how she would have responded if he had. Would she have run away as she had last time? Would she have stayed? Would she have considered seeing where the physical attraction would lead them this time?

But the depth of emotion he had seen in her eyes, with tears streaking down her cheeks after they'd told Lizzie who he was—*that* had done the most damage to his original resolve not to get involved with her again, hadn't it? Maybe that was when it had happened.

'We never burn dinner,' Lizzie complained.

'Well, don't start now.' She glanced at him again as she left the room.

Oh, yes, she *knew* he wasn't done with her. So he winked at Lizzie. 'I'll be right back and you're in charge of the dinner.'

Rhiannon was almost on the first landing as he came out of the kitchen, her shoulders slumped, head bowed as she took each step.

He took the stairs two at a time. 'Wait a minute.'

Her shoulders rose before she turned, her eyes guarded. And Kane hated that. He'd thought they were getting past that stage.

'I thought you were going to watch dinner.'

'I didn't know your parents turned you away.'

'Why would you have; you weren't—'

'*There*? I know. It would have been better if I had been, I can promise you that.'

She frowned hard and glanced up the landing, almost as if she was wishing there was an escape route. 'It worked out fine in the end.'

He stepped closer, a part of him desperately wanting to take the dull tone from her voice. '"Fine". You use that word a lot, don't you?'

Confusion clouded her eyes for a moment. 'Yes, fine. I don't understand the problem with the word. It was—' she enunciated the word with a little more deliberation '—*fine*, as in not a problem. We got through. Just like now—everything is fine—it's working out, isn't it?'

He opened his mouth to answer that but, before he could say a word, she frowned and added, in a softer tone, 'Thank you for the way you were with Lizzie. I can't possibly feel any worse about keeping you both apart, especially after today. If it helps any knowing it, there's nothing you can do or say to punish me more than I'm already punishing myself for that mistake.'

'I don't want to punish you, Mac.' He reached out for her hand, his thumb grazing back and forth against the beating pulse below the soft skin of her wrist. 'And I don't think you should punish yourself any more either. I understand why you hated me when you did, and I think we can both look back on it all now and make more sense of the mistakes we both made. It's done. And now we're—'

'Fine?' She smiled a very small smile before her chin dropped and she studied his hand holding hers.

Kane smiled at the top of her head, his eyes following some of the deeper strands of red. And for the first time in a very long time he was at a loss for words.

But not managing to find what he wanted to say—in all likelihood because he didn't actually know *what* it was he wanted to say—gave Rhiannon cause to break the awkward silence by extricating her hand from his. And when her chin rose she had a brighter smile pinned on her face and a shield across her eyes that stopped him from reading her thoughts.

A wave of something resembling fear crossed his chest before she spoke. 'I'm glad this happened, I really am. I want you to know that, Kane.'

'I am too.'

She nodded. 'We've laid all the ghosts to rest now.'

His eyes narrowed at the statement, as if somehow by shutting a door on the past he sensed she was closing some kind of a door on the future too. When he wanted—

Hell. He didn't know what he wanted. She had an innate ability to pull the rug out from underneath his feet. And, just to add to his sense of frustration at that fact, she then reached out and patted his arm. *Patted his arm*—as of he was some kind of elderly relative or the damn dog!

'I'm glad we can be friends again.'

Kane frowned. 'And when exactly were we *friends*?'

Her long lashes flickered as she focused on a point past his shoulder. 'I think it's important we be friends now—for Lizzie's sake.'

For Lizzie's sake. It was a phrase he'd used all too often himself, but suddenly it didn't seem enough any more; there had to be…*more*…

'Well, yes, I agree b—'

She smiled the overly bright smile again. 'And the fact that we can communicate so well can only help with the decisions we'll probably have to make down the line, as parents.'

Kane pursed his lips, shoving his hands deep into his pockets in an attempt not to reach out and shake her. Because he *really* wanted to shake her! What was she doing? Not that everything she'd said didn't make a certain amount of sense, but—

She wasn't done. 'I know you'll need to go back to your own life soon, now that everything is sorted out. So maybe tomorrow we can talk about when you want to have Lizzie come to you or when you'd like to come visit here. Just so we both know where we're at.'

More practicalities and he agreed with all of that too, he did. It made perfect sense. It was pretty much the way he'd thought things would work out once everything was in the open. So why in hell did it feel like some kind of rejection?

Had he let himself get too comfortable at Brookfield? Was that all it was? It was true; they'd slipped into a kind of comfortable routine of late, despite the times when Rhiannon and he parted ways during the day to do their work. But then most couples spent some time apart during the day when they were working, didn't they?

Whoa. Now they were a couple in his mind?

He rocked back a little from her while he tried to quantify exactly what it was they were. They'd never at any stage been just friends. They weren't a couple. They most definitely weren't lovers any more, no matter how the memories of that time had been plaguing his thoughts of late—day and night. Especially since that one damn kiss he'd so very nearly repeated…

So what in hell were they?

Lizzie's parents—yes—but they were hardly two strangers who would work separately to raise her. At least, he didn't want them to be. That would make them two separate halves of one family. And, back in the days when he had actually allowed himself to think about a family in his future, that just wasn't the way he'd envisaged it being. But in order to be a family there had to be something more, didn't there?

He was still frowning when she spoke again, her gaze rising to look into his eyes. 'There's no need to feel guilty about leaving, you know—not when she'll know you're coming back. Your company is important to you; you've spent years building it up and you've been away from it for nearly a month now.'

It really would help him to sort his thoughts out if she'd just stop being so damn reasonable!

'I'm just going to come right out with this—bear with me, okay?'

All right—because if one of them maybe knew how they felt that would be helpful.

She took a breath. 'I know some people might have sat down and lived off the money their family left them, but you didn't do that.' She smiled a smaller, more genuine smile that made it all the way up into her eyes, softening them so that the warmth radiated across to him. 'And I think that's a wonderful example you've set our daughter.'

He shrugged off the words that should really have made him feel at least a certain amount of pride, because he had a sneaking suspicion he wasn't going to like where she was heading. 'I'm not the only guy in the world to have done that.'

'No, but you're maybe one of the few who felt they'd something to prove after being sick so early on, aren't you? I know you well enough now to know that some kind of control over *something* would have been important to you, wouldn't it?'

How in hell did she know that?

She stepped closer, her chin rising so that she could continue looking into his eyes. And Kane held his breath, his heart thundering loudly as he attempted to hold himself under control.

She may have a better idea of why he'd done some of the things he had back in the day but she really had no idea just how much she was testing him by being so close to him, did she?

It would take so little effort to unclench the fists currently held in his pockets, to reach for her, to haul her into his arms and kiss her senseless until she understood just how far they fell from the 'friends' description. But in doing that he would be moving them on to territory that would involve the 'more' that he hadn't quite got figured out yet. And if he couldn't figure that part out, then what in hell would he say to her? Because he doubted very much that a passionate affair like their last one would be enough this time round—not now that there were so many added complications—like their child and the fact that they were, technically speaking, business partners with the house and the estate.

Before he knew it, she laid one slender hand on his chest, right above his thundering heart, and the ache inside him was so powerful he almost groaned aloud. She really was pushing him to the limit.

'I just want you to know you don't have to prove anything to Lizzie. She loves you. You're an amazing father already. So you don't have to bury yourself in your work any more, thinking up games for all those millions of kids while convinced you'll never have any of your own. You have her. One day you'll have more—'

Right—enough was enough! He had one hand unclenched and out of his pocket in the blink of an eye, clasping her hand tightly as he pulled it off his chest. 'I don't need you to give me a pep talk.'

'I know you don't.'

He placed her hand back at her side and released it, a combination of frustration and confusion fuelling his rising anger. 'You're right, I do need to get back to work; I've been here longer than I planned. But it needed doing—' he clenched his jaw '—for Lizzie's sake.'

He leaned his head a little closer to add, 'But I won't have you feeling sorry for me, Rhiannon—just be quite clear on that.'

Her eyes widened, her mouth gaped open and then she completely stunned him by laughing, albeit a little nervously. 'You idiot. I don't feel sorry for you.'

Kane stared down at her in stark amazement. He'd thought he could read this woman's thoughts? He hadn't a clue how her mind worked!

'The irony is I don't think I've ever had so much respect for anyone. You're the strongest person I know. You faced and fought your illness, you built a business from the ground up when you really didn't have to go to all that effort, you've come down here and in the space of a single month shown what a terrific father you can be—not to mention turning every opinion I ever had of you right on its head—' She shook her head, focused again on the same point just past his shoulder. 'I don't feel the least bit sorry for you, Kane Healey. Not one little bit.'

She looked back into his eyes and again he was at a complete loss for words.

'All I was *trying* to say was that you have nothing to prove. Not to anyone. But you don't need to bury yourself in your work to compensate for anything either. You already have a family, even if you'd told yourself you'd never have one.' She smiled, her voice husky. 'Lizzie *is* your family.'

He ran his hand roughly over his hair and down his face as she turned and walked away, shaking his head as he tried to take in everything she'd just said and to untangle how he felt. And she was halfway up the second flight of stairs before he found some husky words of his own.

'Sometimes I think you don't know me at all—and then

sometimes I think you know me better than anyone else ever has. I don't know how I feel about that.'

'Well, when you do we can maybe have a talk about it. That's what being friends is all about.'

CHAPTER TWELVE

IF SOMEONE had told her just over a month ago that she'd miss Kane when he left she'd have laughed herself silly.

Thankfully she had the preparations for the Valentine Ball to occupy her between the brief times she got to hear his voice on the phone when he called Lizzie. Not that he didn't always take the time to enquire how she was, or how she was getting on with the combined running of the house and the estate, the latter of which he had been happy to let her look after when he was away—and she could consult with him if she needed to—that was all *fine*.

But *fine* really wasn't enough any more. In fact, fine would probably never be enough again. Not now that she'd had a glimpse into what might have been. And having Kane as a part of Lizzie's life, living under the same roof as them both so they looked like a happy family to the outside world, had left Rhiannon with a permanent sense of loss for that 'might have been'.

But it wasn't just that—it was *him*. She missed *him*. The sound of his voice, his deep laughter, the way her pulse would skip when he looked at her with his gorgeous blue eyes. And he was so much more than she'd ever thought anyone could be—strong in character as well as body, braver than probably even he thought he was and with an ability to care so very deeply, the way he did for Lizzie—all adding together to make him exactly the kind of man she'd once believed he might be.

So that having lost him back then, and not having him with her *that way* now, was just the most extreme form of agony she had ever felt. She might not have been in love before, but she was in love now, wasn't she?

For some reason it was the night of the Ball that she missed him most. And she couldn't just put it down to the fact that she was one of the very few there without a partner.

Everywhere she looked, the house was alive with people, laughter, soft lights, the scent of flowers and the sound of music. But she couldn't enjoy the fact that it felt as if Brookfield had finally come back to life because, even surrounded by so many people, she was still alone—because Kane wasn't there to share it.

She wasn't even thirty years old yet and it felt as if she were facing the rest of her life alone. There was still time to meet someone, she reasoned, but whoever it was wouldn't be *him*. He was going to take some getting over. And knowing that she'd have to see him, spend time with him, watch him with their daughter, all from the sidelines… Well, it was going to be complete torture, wasn't it?

Walking down the hall with her hostess smile firmly in place, she caught sight of herself in one of the huge gilt mirrors. She'd taken a lot of time and effort with how she looked, all too aware of the place she now had in the local community and the need to at least do *something* right. So she took a moment to smooth her hands down over the pale gold of her long empire-line dress, to check that all of her curls were still pinned up in the right places, that none of the curl in the longer strands brushing her shoulders had dropped out.

And then she glanced briefly at her make-up and was

stunned by the sadness she could see in her own eyes. Could everyone see how miserable she was? Damn him! It would be so much easier if she could still hate him.

She straightened the pearl choker at her neck and turned, to look straight up into familiar blue eyes.

'Lizzie told me there was a party somewhere.'

Oh, hell. He looked *amazing*! How was that fair?

She dragged her gaze from his eyes to make an inventory of what he was wearing, deciding in a heartbeat that he should spend every day of the rest of his life in a dinner jacket and a bow-tie. He just—filled it—better than any other man she'd seen in the same outfit that evening, even if he had the jacket unbuttoned and his hands deep in his pockets.

Actually, on reflection, there was something incredibly sexy about *that* too.

She bit her bottom lip, lifting her chin as he approached. 'I didn't know you were part of the local Hunt Club.'

'My daughter invited me. She said she had a new dress that I had to see "and everything".'

Rhiannon's gaze softened when he smiled a slow, ridiculously sexy smile. 'She's gorgeous in it.'

'I bet she is.'

But he didn't ask where Lizzie was or make an attempt to find her. And eventually Rhiannon couldn't take just standing there looking at him while that silent, almost *knowing* gleam shone in his eyes, even if she felt almost maniacally happy to see him.

'Can I get you a drink of something?'

Kane chuckled at her polite sweeping wave of one hand. 'Well, you're obviously very comfortable in the role of hostess.'

'As a matter of fact, I am.' She smiled more openly—couldn't seem to stop herself from smiling, as it happened. Then she looked up and around the huge hall. 'But you have to admit that Brookfield is an amazing setting. Just look at it, it was meant for this kind of thing. I don't think it's ever looked more beautiful.'

When she looked back into his eyes he smiled again, then looked slowly down over her dress and back up. 'Yes, beautiful is the right word.'

Rhiannon's breath caught. What was *that*?

She swallowed again. 'There's, um, there's still some food left from the buffet, I think, that is, if you're hungry. It's through here—'

She tore her gaze from his, aware that heat was rising on her cheeks as she stepped to one side to show him where the buffet was set up. But, without moving from the same place, he took a hand from his pocket and captured hers, his long, warm fingers immediately tangling with hers.

'Dance with me.'

His hand felt wonderful. And yes, she was fully aware that he'd just walked in unannounced, looking the way he did, and she'd pretty much reacted like a shy teenager with a crush, but she needed the physical contact. She needed to be with him like this, to let her guard down enough to prove to herself that she could still get along with him, spend time with him and not allow the fact that she was in love with him to get in the way.

So she turned her head and looked up at him with a challenging quirk of her eyebrows. 'How do I even know you can dance? You might have two left feet.'

Kane turned round, switching his hands as he leaned a little closer to her face, his deep voice low and deliciously seductive. 'Let's find out, shall we?'

Rhiannon let him guide her through the crowd to the sitting room, where all of the furniture had been cleared to turn it into a mini ballroom. And when they were surrounded by swaying couples he turned and drew her forward into his arms, waiting until her hands rose to clasp behind his neck before he drew her closer and began to sway them to the music.

Rhiannon let her thumbs brush against the short hair at the nape of his neck; she breathed in the hint of cinnamon, relaxed back on to the band of his arms and couldn't, for the life of her, tear her gaze from his.

She was officially smitten.

But it was perfect. And surely she couldn't be damned forever for wanting one perfect moment with him?

He smiled another slow, sensual smile with the kind of warmth she felt seep in to melt her bones.

'See, I don't have two left feet.'

She smiled back at him. 'Its early days.'

'Time will tell.' He leaned a little closer. 'How come we've never danced together before?'

Oh, they'd danced. They'd danced more than he probably realized. It felt as if she'd spent most of her life dancing *with* him and *around* him.

'We did that seventies disco night that one time.'

He laughed, his large hands flattening against her back, smoothing the material over her skin in small, slow, gentle sweeps. 'Ah, but back then, with us, that wasn't dancing. It was foreplay.'

With her hips swaying in time with his, Rhiannon wasn't entirely convinced that what they were currently doing wasn't exactly the same thing. Telling herself she'd blame the three glasses of wine she'd had when she looked back on it all in the morning, she didn't try to brush aside what he'd said or make a sarcastic comment in reply. Instead, she simply looked at him from beneath lowered lashes, damping her lips before she told him, 'You had a very one track mind back then.'

Kane grumbled his reply. 'Only because you were a bad influence on me.'

'I remember how much persuasion it took.'

He nodded, his hands continuing their slow smoothing over her back. 'I guess, considering the law of percentages, we were always likely to have a chance of making a Lizzie, weren't we?'

'Yes.' The word was almost a whisper. 'Nothing is ever a one hundred per cent guarantee.'

'No. But sometimes, even when we know that, we still take a chance. Maybe there's just no stopping something that's meant to be.' He drew her in closer as he spoke, so that the last words were said directly above her ear.

Rhiannon's eyelids grew heavy so she closed her eyes, surrendering to the waves of sensuality, while her heart ached all over again for what she couldn't have. It'd been like this last time, hadn't it? Maybe it had even been the start of what she felt now. Had she been falling in love back then and not realized? Was that why she'd fallen so quickly this time?

'Sometimes it's worth having a little faith that things will eventually work out the way they're supposed to, no matter what mistakes we make along the way.'

Rhiannon's eyes opened and she frowned. What did he mean by that? Was she starting to imagine that he was hinting at something he wasn't because she wanted him to want more? But, when she leaned back against his arms to try and read his expression, he was looking over her head.

'Aha, I see my daughter. And you're right, she does look gorgeous.' He flashed a smile over at Lizzie. 'I'd better go dance with her too.'

Rhiannon nodded, her brain still feeling fluffy. 'I think she'd love that.'

He leaned back, dropping his chin to look into her eyes. 'I'm glad we're friends now, Mac.'

Her own words. And he may as well have stabbed her in the chest. It certainly couldn't have hurt any less. But she managed to nod again, to smile a small smile, even if she had to look away from his eyes to do it. 'Me too.'

He released her, stepped sideways and then completely surprised her, twisting the knife at the same time, by placing a soft, fleeting kiss against her cheek before stage whispering into her ear, 'And, just in case I haven't already said it: you look very beautiful tonight. But then you were always beautiful.'

Rhiannon stood in the centre of the dance floor for a moment so she could blink back the tears that had formed at the back of her eyes, so that she could swallow hard and take a couple of deep breaths, to gain control before she pinned her hostess smile back on.

How in hell was she going to get through this?

She moved back into the crowd, shaking hands with people, listening to stories about Brookfield and Mattie's family. And then, halfway between two groups, she caught sight of Kane escorting Lizzie to the dance floor so she slipped back a little to watch.

He bowed, Lizzie giggled and Rhiannon smiled affectionately at them both. They were just so very alike—the two people she loved the most.

She swallowed hard, tears stinging her eyes again, while Kane lifted Lizzie up into his arms, her slender arms around his neck and legs swinging below his waist as they started to dance. It was the most beautiful thing Rhiannon had ever seen—heartbreakingly beautiful. And agonizing—because the need to walk over and join them, to dance with Kane with Lizzie held between them—was so strong it almost killed her.

This was the way her life was going to be from now on—standing on the outside looking in. And if it weren't for the seventy guests in her house she'd have disappeared upstairs so she didn't have to watch it.

Yet another deep breath, yet another lift of her chin, because she had to get on with it, didn't she? Standing and watching wasn't going to feel any better after ten minutes.

And she managed it, just. She got through the rest of the evening, even though she was constantly aware of where Kane was at any given time, of the people he was talking to—particularly the women—of the sound of his voice when he was close by or his scent as he walked past. And she even managed to smile across at him when he looked at her. But, as the night drew to a close and they stood side by side at the front doors waving goodbye to the last of the guests, watching their cars circle as they drove off the gravel, Rhiannon felt her mouth go dry, her heart beat a little louder, felt that no matter how many breaths she took she couldn't seem to get enough air into her lungs.

The door clicked shut and she rested her palm on its cool surface for a moment before turning round and flashing a small smile at him. 'I'll have to go check that Lizzie actually went to bed when I sent her an hour ago. Any clearing up can wait till the morning.'

'I checked; she's out for the count. You throw a hell of a party, Mac.'

Half of her really wished he would stop using the old nickname. It didn't help any. But then neither did his falling into step beside her as she walked to the staircase.

'Well, I did have some help from the Committee. They're an enthusiastic bunch.' She lifted her long skirt to negotiate the stairs, her focus on her feet so that she didn't notice him reaching out for her elbow until the searing heat of his touch burnt her skin.

When her breath caught his fingers tightened. 'Lizzie told me you arranged most of it, though, right down to the colours of the flowers and moving furniture under your own steam.'

She swallowed hard and tried to concentrate on not tripping. 'It all came together in the end.'

His warm fingers eased a little against her elbow, widened, smoothed over her skin in a caress she felt clean to the soles of her feet. Didn't he have *any* idea what he was doing to her?

But when they reached the landing and Rhiannon tried to gently pull her elbow free, he froze her to the spot with a flat toned, 'Did you love Stephen?'

'What?' Her head rose sharply. Where had that come from? 'Did you?'

'Why?' Rhiannon really didn't see what it had to do with anything. And she certainly didn't want to stand and confess to the man she'd made the biggest mistake of her life with, the details of the second biggest mistake she'd ever made.

He confused her even further by smiling wryly, his blue eyes studying her face intently. 'Because I think when I knew you'd married him was when I started hating you as much as you hated me.'

It was the very last thing she would ever have expected him to say and yet a part of her almost shouted with joy at the very idea of him being jealous. Which was ridiculous—it wasn't what he was saying, was it?

'It had nothing to do with you by then.'

'No, but it still bugged the hell out of me.'

Oh, she knew what he was saying now. And it was yet another twist of the damn knife! So she turned away as she spoke, determined she wouldn't show him how much he'd just hurt her. 'Because you thought Lizzie was his and that meant I had to have been with him right after I was with you, that's why. We already covered all that.'

He reached for her elbow again, tugged her round and then marched her backwards until she had her back against the wall. And when Rhiannon let go of her skirt, he took hold of both of her wrists, his thumbs moving back and forth against her erratic pulse. 'Yes, that was one element of it. But hell, Mac, it was

Stephen—it was a constant competition for him to have what was mine. I thought you knew that.'

Her heart caught on the 'what was mine'. Was that how he'd thought of her then? She searched his eyes for the answer and found him searching her eyes the same way, the air crackling between them.

'It had nothing to do with me marrying him.'

'Then make me understand.'

She was completely distracted by the movement of his thumbs on her wrists, so it took a moment for her to weigh up the pros and cons of telling him the truth.

His mouth curled into another devastating smile. 'And now you're trying to decide whether or not to be honest with me, aren't you?'

'Do you have any idea how annoying it is when you do that? I mean, *really*?'

'I seem to remember there were times when you liked that I knew what you were thinking.'

The words were pure seduction, especially when she knew *exactly* what he was talking about. 'That was different. That had to do with the whole physical thing we had going.'

His voice dropped an octave. 'Don't worry, we'll get to that subject in a minute.'

Rhiannon swallowed a moan. She really couldn't take much more of this. She couldn't! And why in hell was he putting her through it?

'Did you love him?'

'No!' She threw the answer at him. 'There—happy now?'

He tilted his head to one side, shrugging his broad shoulders. 'It's a start. So if you didn't love him, then why did you marry him?'

If she stood there much longer she was going to cry in front of him, she really was. So she tugged her wrists and scowled at him when he wouldn't set her free. All right, he wanted to know why, then she'd damn well tell him why!

'Fine, then. If you really want to know, it was because *he* wanted to marry *me*!'

The hold on her wrists tightened as he swore under his breath. And immediately Rhiannon pushed off the wall, standing on tiptoe to bring her face closer to his. 'And now you think he only wanted that to get at you in some way? Grow up, Kane! He was there and you weren't. He wanted to be with me and you didn't. It was nothing to do with you! And frankly, it still isn't, so let me go!'

'Did *he* love *you*?'

'Is that so very hard for you to believe?'

The steady tone of his answer did her in. 'No, that I could understand a lot better now that I actually know you. I wouldn't blame him for feeling that.'

What did he mean by that? Because there was no way in hell he meant… This was *insane*! She shook her head.

'You're unbelievable. And they say *women* twist things.'

Out of nowhere, he released her hands. But, as she looked down in surprise, both of his hands rose to her waist and he stepped forward, pinning her back against the wall again so that the entire length of his hard, heated body was pressed intimately against hers.

It was like setting a match to touch paper.

Her blood rushed faster through her veins. Her heart pumped harder to help the blood to move at the increased speed. She wanted him *so* badly!

'So you married him because he loved you, and because you were alone, and because you had a baby to support. You married him for security, right?'

'I didn't give a damn about his money, if that's what you mean.' Her words were breathless, her breasts rising and falling rapidly as she fought for air. And if the truth was the only escape route she had, then she had to take it. 'I could have supported Lizzie, I'd done it up until then. He wasn't as bad as you think he was. He was charming and funny and *uncomplicated*. And when he asked me to marry him, I told myself that it was better to go into marriage without love as the basis for it. Or, or—*this*—this thing *we* had.'

'No love and no—*this*?' His voice dropped. 'Because it was safer that way?'

'Maybe—partly—I don't know. But it doesn't matter now.'

His fingers spread wide against her waist, his thumbs brushing against the bottom of her ribcage as he tilted his face over hers, his eyes even more intense close up. 'No love so you couldn't get hurt—'

'Love doesn't guarantee a marriage will last.'

His gaze dropped to her parted lips as he moved his hands along her sides, drawing another gasp from her. 'And no *this*—because?'

'Because *this* doesn't last—when I'm ninety and grey-haired and round-shouldered, even *we* wouldn't still have this.'

His gaze rose, the pupils of his eyes large and dark, his voice huskier. 'Oh, I don't know. I think *we'd* still have *this*. It certainly hasn't gone away, has it? When I'm ninety-three, grey-haired and round-shouldered, I think I'd still give it my best shot.'

And talk like that just made her heart ache all the more. 'It's still not enough on its own.'

'All right, what more is there?'

'Like I'd know.' She laughed nervously, feeling herself on the edge of a mildly panicky hysteria. 'In case you hadn't noticed, my track record isn't very good. If you need tips for future reference you'd be better asking someone who hasn't discovered that they do much better on their own.'

'You married the wrong man, that's all.' When her eyes

widened at the statement, he leaned his head a little closer, his breath fanning out over her heated cheeks. 'And you *didn't* have *this* with *him*.'

There was nothing beyond the kiss; no sound barring their deep breathing, no light barring the ones that danced behind her eyelids, nothing that wasn't completely focused on his firm mouth moving against her soft lips.

She was drowning in him.

He traced his lips along hers, added a little pressure, tugged on her bottom lip until she opened her mouth on a low moan and he deepened the kiss, coaxing her tongue to dance with his.

It wasn't fair. She couldn't do this again—not the physical *alone*. This time she wanted more from him. And there was just too much history. Try as they might, the mistakes would always be there. The mistakes that would open up cracks in any relationship they tried and eventually drive them apart.

And Rhiannon knew she wouldn't survive it this time.

Kane tore his mouth from hers, his face still close as he searched her eyes. 'A lot of people don't even have this, you know. And we have more than this already. We have a child. Is that enough, do you think?'

What did he mean? He couldn't possibly mean…?

It took a split second for it to sink in. 'You can't be serious. You're suggesting some kind of a—what is it called—?' she stared up at him in disbelief '—marriage of convenience? You honestly think I'd ever consider that—with *you*?'

He scowled. 'Why not with me?'

'I can't believe you think I'd even consider it. With one failed marriage behind me, do you honestly think I'd enter into that kind of a *farce*? What the hell century do you think we live in?'

He stepped back from her. 'All along we've said for Liz—'

'*O-oh* no!' She waggled a finger at him when she had enough space, her eyes blazing with hurt, anger and a rapidly growing sense of humiliation. 'Don't you dare use the "for Lizzie's sake" line! I'm more than capable of looking after her on my own. I'll do whatever it takes for her to get to spend time with you, but that's only because you're a different person with her than you are with me.'

And that killed her above all else. He could love his child unconditionally and yet still think that a loveless marriage would be something her mother would consider! When there was just no way she could do it. And, even if she could, she couldn't with *him*. Not when she loved him like she did.

Tears glittered in her eyes as she laid it all on the line for him. 'The Kane Healey I saw dancing with his daughter tonight is a thousand times more of a man than the one who stood here right this minute! He's this amazing guy who doesn't have a problem with showing how much he loves her, even after so little time. If I ever married again it would be for a whole combination of things and part of that *would* be love—it would have to be, for me. And it's not here, so never in *a million years* would I ever marry you.'

He had the gall to look amused. 'A million years?'

'Yes! A million years.' She hiccupped on the words and stepped forward, lifting both hands to shove against his chest. 'Get the hell away from me. I take back every nice thought I've had about you since I got to know you this time round.'

'What kind of nice thoughts?'

She shoved him again. 'I was dumb enough to think you were much more than I'd realized first time around.' Another shove, and each one took him back a step until he had his back against the wooden banister, where she laughed in his face. 'I was even stupid enough to find it weird around here without you! But now I'm glad you left!'

His eyes turned a darker shade of blue, his mouth lifting into the softest smile she had ever seen, one that almost looked affectionate, but she knew was amusement again because she'd just given him yet another victory, hadn't she?

'Mac—' The nickname came out with a husky edge.

'And don't you dare call me that! I hate you!'

'No, you don't.'

She laughed again, sarcastically this time. 'Right this second I do! You might not have managed to completely break my heart the first time round, but you're close to managing it *this time*. If you gave a damn about me, even as Lizzie's mother, then you'd care about my chance at happiness!'

Grabbing her skirt in two fists, she turned on her heel and ran up the next flight of stairs, determined to get to her bedroom and lock the door before he could stop her. But he didn't follow her. He didn't make any attempt to stop her or to tell her she'd got him wrong. Or even to say that she deserved a chance to be happy.

And she *did* genuinely hate him for that.

CHAPTER THIRTEEN

KANE needed to find a way to get Rhiannon to talk to him again. And fast. Because the longer he let it fester, the harder she would be to persuade that he'd simply got his approach wrong the night before.

It was her damn fault, after all. If she didn't have him so sideways most of the time then he'd have made a better job of it! But oh, no, last night she had floored him the second he'd laid eyes on her. Ten years ago they'd have lasted five minutes at that party!

Then there'd been the dance and finally holding her in his arms when he'd done nothing but think about holding her again since he'd left. Damn her—even the five minutes he got to talk to her on the phone each time he called Lizzie had been proving the highlight of his day of late. He was obsessed by her. And that had made him look more closely at how he'd felt about her the first time around. Had he been in love and not known it? There was no way of knowing, but it would be a rational explanation for the fact that he'd felt so much so fast this time round. He'd felt every emotion going since meeting her again. And he hadn't known what it all meant, not really, not until he was away from her and from Lizzie—*his family*. He'd missed them—*both of them*—more than he would ever have thought it possible to miss anyone.

But it had taken Rhiannon to stand there in *that dress*, looking as beautiful as she did, with a frame of soft lights and flowers behind her, for him to have what he already knew confirmed. Yes, he knew what the elusive *something more* was now...

Now all he had to do was put it right.

After several hours tossing and turning in the wee small hours, while he fought the urge to storm down the hall and convince her the old-fashioned way that she'd misread what he was trying to say, a tiny seed of an idea came to him. By six-thirty it was a full-blown plan. Then all he had to do was hire an accomplice...

When Lizzie announced she was going to make dinner on her own, Rhiannon escaped to her room to take a break from the constant smiling she'd been forced to do all day long. She'd done everything to avoid spending time with Kane—everything. She'd put the furniture back, cleared up—and there was a lot to clear up!—and hoovered and dusted. She hadn't even stopped for lunch. The theory being that the busier she stayed then the sooner the day would be over and he'd be gone again.

Something she prayed would happen *very soon* when she caught glimpses of him with Lizzie during the day—laughing, smiling and hugging when the notion struck them. They were *both* torturing her and it *hurt*.

But after a long soak in the bath, when she felt capable of facing them both again, she found a picture pinned to the kitchen door with Lizzie's multicoloured handwriting telling her it was out of bounds.

A tingling on the back of her neck told her Kane was nearby. 'Apparently we're not allowed in the kitchen.'

He walked over to stand beside her, his arms folded across

his chest as he dropped his chin to read the note, frowning at it. 'I wonder what she's up to?'

Rhiannon sighed. 'I have no idea.'

They both stood there for another minute, until the ache in her chest started to demand her attention again. She was too emotionally drained to play games with Lizzie. 'I might just skip dinner. I'm still tired after last night.'

'You should eat something. You skipped lunch.' He knocked on the door, his voice rising, 'Can we come in?'

'*No!*'

Rhiannon sighed again. 'Have you any idea *when*?'

The door swung open and Lizzie stepped through, closing it behind her. Both of her parents stared at her before Kane asked, 'What's in your hair?'

She lifted a hand, swiped at it and then sucked it off her finger. 'Mayonnaise.'

Kane nodded. 'Of course it is.'

'You aren't having dinner in the kitchen; you're having it in the stove room. Come on.'

Oh, Rhiannon *so* didn't want to play, not today, but a glance at Kane, who quirked his dark brows in challenge, was enough to galvanize her. She'd be damned if he took anything more from her than he already had! So she followed Lizzie down the slope to the stove room, unprepared for what she found when she got there.

'What *is* this?'

The room was bedecked with various crêpe paper and cardboard hearts and pink paper chains. The hexagonal table underneath the window was set for two, with paper cups covered in yet more hearts and a single daffodil beside a candle.

Lizzie beamed up at them both after Kane ducked his head under the door frame. 'Happy Valentine's Day!'

Oh, no. Rhiannon could have curled up and died.

Kane leaned closer to ask her in a stage whisper, 'Did you know it was still Valentine's Day?'

Frowning hard, she shook her head, then stopped. 'Well, actually, yes, I suppose I did. The Ball was a day early because it couldn't be on a Sunday when most people have work on Monday and…'

Her words petered out as a thought occurred to her and she scowled up at him. 'I had nothing to do with this.'

He smiled. 'I know.'

'Mum, you sit over that side—' Lizzie pointed at the far chair '—and Dad, you sit here.'

It was the first time she'd called him Dad. They both turned to look at her, then back at each other with a shared smile of understanding at the importance of the one tiny word. It was a bittersweet moment for Rhiannon.

'Maybe we should just humour her?'

But it didn't feel any less dreadful to Rhiannon when they were sitting at the table and Lizzie handed matches to Kane. 'You have to light the candle. It's more romantic that way.'

Rhiannon moaned a low moan, resting her elbow on the table so she could hide her eyes behind her hand. She heard the door close and then a deep chuckle.

'This is nice.'

'I'm glad you think so.' She glared at him from behind her open fingers. 'You do know what she's doing?'

He grinned, resting his forearms on the table so he could lean forward, his voice still low. 'Yes, I know *exactly* what she's doing.'

Rhiannon moaned again and dropped her forehead on to the table. 'I really don't know how much more of these twenty-four hours I can take.' She continued in a muffled voice, feeling sick to her stomach, 'We can't let her think this will lead to anything. You'll have to talk to her.'

She heard him chuckle again.

'Why do *I* have to talk to her?'

Because her mother didn't think she could look her in the eyes and tell her that she didn't love her father that way, that was why, even when she currently hated his guts. Flip side of the same thing, she guessed... And, in fairness, it had always been that way—he'd always been able to make her as mad as a hatter with a few sentences. The only difference back then had been how he'd made it up to her afterwards.

She lifted her head and frowned at him. 'Well, *we're* not going to let her think—'

The door opened and Lizzie backed in, turning round to set a plate in front of each of them. 'Starters.'

Kane took one look at Rhiannon's face when Lizzie left and dissolved into raucous laughter, which she rewarded with another glare. 'Oh, I'm *so* glad *one of us* is enjoying this!'

'You'd be amused too if you could see the expression on your face.'

'It's not funny!'

'Oh, come on, it's a little bit funny. And romantic in an off the wall way, don't you think?'

He swallowed down his laughter when she aimed another glare his way, lifting a fork to play with the contents of his plate. 'What do you think it is?'

After a moment's debate on the merits of running away, Rhiannon lifted her fork and dug around, eventually rolling out an egg. 'Egg mayonnaise.'

'There's an egg in there?'

'Yes, a whole entire round boiled egg.' She glanced up at him and couldn't help but smile a small smile. He then smiled back, which helped some, but still... 'Seriously, we can't let her do this. She's trying to matchmake.'

Kane nodded. 'Well, you can't really blame her.'

'And what does *that* mean?'

He shrugged, his gaze dropping to focus on finding his egg. 'She's a smart kid; we both know that. And she's bound to have seen how we are together.'

'What do you mean, *how we are together*? We're not any *way* when we're together.'

His thick lashes rose, a glint of humour in his blue eyes. 'Now, that wouldn't be entirely true, would it?' He nodded at her plate. 'You'd better eat some of that or you'll hurt her feelings.'

Rhiannon honestly thought she'd choke on it. Whereas Kane had no difficulty whatsoever in tucking into his. 'You think she knows that we—?'

His brows quirked as he spoke with his mouth still half full. 'Kissed? Almost kissed? Which time do you want to discuss?'

She opened her mouth to say something cutting, but nothing came out. So she closed it again. Realistically, she was digging a bigger hole for herself every time, wasn't she?

'Eat something.'

She speared a piece of cucumber and popped it in her mouth, smirking sarcastically at him as she chewed.

'Now, Mac, don't go ruining a romantic evening by being petulant; it's Valentine's Day.' He reached across the table and stole her egg. 'The least you can do is make it look like you ate some of it; move it about on the plate or something.'

Lizzie reappeared. 'Lift your plates, please.'

She set two larger plates down and took the smaller ones from them. 'I put in more salad 'cos Mum always says it's good for you.'

Kane nodded, a better disguised smile on his face. 'It's lovely, sweetheart. You've done a great job.'

When Lizzie beamed at his praise, Rhiannon immediately felt guilty. 'It is, really. You've worked *very* hard on this.'

'But there's nothing green in the dessert, right?'

Even Rhiannon couldn't help chuckling at his question, but

she still kicked him under the table for it, his small flinch deeply satisfying, because she *really* wanted to stay mad with him. She didn't want to laugh with him again. Mad was easier. Mad had no hopes or dreams. Mad knew exactly where it stood.

'I'm only teasing. I'm sure it'll be lovely.'

'It's ice cream.'

'I love ice cream.'

'Me too.' Lizzie grinned and winked at him.

Kane winked back and Rhiannon had to shake her head to shift the ridiculous notion that in some way he approved of what she was doing.

'And you have to talk to each other.'

'We will.'

Right, she'd had about enough. So she called him on it when Lizzie left. 'We're *telling* her.'

She didn't look at him as she said it. Looking at him had a bad effect on her heart rate, even when she was mad. So she searched her plate for something to eat to make it look as if she'd made the effort.

Kane's voice rumbled across at her. 'Tell her what?'

'That this isn't going to happen.'

'It already happened.'

'No, it didn't. Not the *it* she's looking to happen.' She set her fork down and scowled at him again, because surely he had to know there was yet another argument looming. 'It's not fair, Kane.'

He stared across at her as he chewed, his blue eyes studying her with the intensity that she always found the most disconcerting. Then he smiled a small smile before he spoke. 'Maybe she just prefers it when we get along, did you think about that? And I happen to agree with that. You were the one who said you were glad we could be *friends*.'

Damn him! Her breath caught at the reminder, her heart

twisting again, and immediately she refocused on her plate, grumbling back between clenched teeth, 'Yes, I did say that.'

'Being friends is important, don't you think?'

She pursed her lips, lifting her fork to push her salad around. 'Of course it is, for Lizzie's sake.'

There was a long silence before he answered, his voice low. 'Not everything has to be for Lizzie's sake.'

Her heart missed several beats. 'Well, no, it doesn't, because we're business partners too, of course—technically speaking.'

'Being able to work together is important too.'

She risked an upward glance in time to see him slowly nodding his head, his gaze still locked on her. And her heart raced a little to make up for the missing beats. What was he *doing*? Hadn't she been clear enough last night?

'And communication is another one. We might need to work on that some.' He looked down at his plate, lifting his knife to slice some ham. 'Though, just for the record, you've always had really expressive eyes. It's why I'm able to guess what you're thinking as often as I do. I always liked that. It was one of my favourite things about you.'

Rhiannon couldn't believe he was saying these things to her *now*—sweet, almost romantic things. Didn't he know what it did to her poor heart? And she felt a shiver of fear run up her spine at the thought of him being able to see how she felt by looking in her eyes. Did he know how she felt about him? How she'd maybe always felt?

If he knew, then he had the advantage. If he chose to he could push her on the marriage of convenience issue. And she'd already learnt the hard way what happened when only one person loved the other.

When he looked up, she focused on her food, clearing her throat before she replied. 'Yes, those things *are* important. I agree with you.'

'That's a first.'

'Don't push it. I already don't like you much at this precise minute, if you remember correctly.'

'I don't think that's entirely true either, is it?'

That got her attention, while he continued in the same steady voice, 'I think you like me more than you're prepared to admit. At least that's what I'm banking on. If I'm wrong, then I'm about to make a real fool of myself here.'

Rhiannon's eye's widened. He *knew*, didn't he?

Lizzie reappeared and Rhiannon groaned, *'Oh, c'mon!'*

'I brought the ice cream.' She set them down. 'And I forgot to turn the music on.'

When she headed for the stereo Rhiannon tried to stop her. 'It's fine, baby; we don't need music.'

'Yes, you do.' She was already selecting a track. 'It's romantic music for you to dance to.'

'I don't want to dance.' The sharp tone drew attention from both of them so she was forced to pin yet another false smile on to her face. 'I'm really tired, Lizzie, that's all. I don't want to dance.'

'I don't have two left feet.'

She glared venomously at him. 'I don't want to dance with you.'

'Is it the wrong music?' Lizzie turned to Kane with a frown. 'You said that track three was the right one.'

He said?

'Yes, it's the right one, don't worry. And you did a great job with the food and decorations, thank you.'

'*You* did this?'

'For Valentine's Day.' Lizzie looked immensely pleased with her father's 'thoughtfulness'. 'It was Dad's idea, but I did all the food by myself.'

Rhiannon tilted her head towards one shoulder and closed her eyes in agony, suddenly breathless and dizzy. When she opened them again Kane was smiling a small smile at her, an incredible softness in his eyes.

Sympathy?

She shook her head in denial, her voice barely above an agonized whisper. 'I can't believe you did this.'

'Your mum and I need to have a talk now. Can you give us a while?'

'Yep.'

Lizzie gave him a hug, planted a smacking kiss on his clean-shaven cheek and then practically skipped out the door—leaving Rhiannon to face Kane alone for what she knew would be the most humiliating moment of her life.

She slumped back in her chair, watching as he pushed his back and stood up. 'I don't believe you did this to me. *Why* did you do this?'

'Take a minute to think about it and you'll figure out why.' He held his hand out to her, palm upward. 'Dance with me.'

'I don't want to dance with you.'

'Yes, you do; we can dance and talk at the same time. And *I* want to dance with *you*.' He lowered his voice. 'Please?'

She gaped at him. Kane never said please. At least she couldn't remember him ever saying it anywhere near *her*. And it was apparently all it took to get her to move. She found herself lifting her hand to slide it into his. She watched as his fingers curled around the back of her hand and at the same time she heard him exhale, as if he had been holding his breath, not quite sure of what she would do.

But that couldn't be right—Kane Healey didn't do unsure, did he?

Bracing on his hand, she pushed her chair back and stood up, allowing him to lead her around the sofa, watching in an almost hypnotic state as he stopped and drew her in against him, still holding on to her hand while his arm snaked around her waist.

Somewhere in the distance she could hear the soft tones of the music in the background but she couldn't have said who was singing. She couldn't focus on anything beyond the gentle swaying that began as her hips fitted in against his. And only then did she lift her chin and look up into his darkening eyes.

'Why are you doing this?'

'You know why.'

'I already told you I wouldn't marry you.'

'In a million years.' He nodded, his eyes sparkling. 'Yes, I remember.'

He continued swaying them, making small steps, beginning to move in a circle at the same time, turning her hand in his so that their fingers were locked together.

'Then why—'

He smiled a smile that curled her toes. 'Still not got it?'

She was afraid to hope, 'I told you I needed more than—'

'This?' He leaned down and brushed his mouth across hers fleetingly, in a whisper of a kiss that spoke of tenderness held within passion.

'Yes.' She closed her eyes as sensation washed over her, all too aware that she was letting him seduce her and unable to fight it as her loosely swinging arm rose to lay her palm on his chest—reaching for a firm anchor she could lean on while the world tilted around her. 'That.'

'You still think that's all there is between us?'

Her eyes fluttered open. 'Isn't it?'

'I plan on proving to you that there's more. And if I don't convince you this time, then I'll keep trying to prove it to you, for as long as it *does* take.'

Rhiannon could feel her heart swelling with hope and it must have shown in her eyes because he smiled again, the look in his eyes reminding her of the day they'd told Lizzie who he was, when he had held her in his arms and hadn't tried to hide how he felt.

Kane raised his brows. 'You're getting it now, aren't you?'

She stared in amazement. 'Keep going.'

They swayed back and forth, circling slowly.

'You said that this on its own wasn't enough.'

'This.' She smiled a very small smile at him and brazenly moved her hips across his in the opposite direction to their swaying, her smile growing when he sucked in a sharp breath. 'Yes, I did say that.'

He shook his head. *'Witch.'*

She smiled all the more, a bubble of happiness growing in the pit of her stomach.

'You also said that having a child together wasn't enough on its own.'

'An *amazing* child.'

'Yes.' His gaze changed, to a sincere intensity tinged with a hint of regret. 'And I need you to be very clear that she's the only one there might ever be with me. Though there are ways to try—'

Did he think that would make a difference to her? If he thought that then he couldn't possibly know how much she loved him, which meant he was taking a chance by doing this. He might not love her as much as she loved him. But she'd figured out that he was saying he wanted to try. There was no way she wasn't taking that chance.

So she lifted the hand she'd been resting on his chest, laying her palm against his cheek as she leaned up on her toes to place the same whisper of a kiss on his mouth, her nose close to his as she informed him in a steady voice, 'That doesn't matter. I already have one amazing child. Yes, a place like Brookfield was meant to be filled with children, and if this worked and we were lucky enough to have another one like Lizzie one day, then that would be more than *fine* with me…'

'For the record—I hate that word—*fine* isn't enough, for any of us.'

No, he was right. It wasn't—not any more. 'With a little work I reckon we could manage better than fine. But if we don't make another Lizzie then you should know I'd still want to fill this place with children for you to be a father to. There's adoption, fostering, we could run camps here in the summer—'

He kissed her into silence, not raising his head until she was breathless. 'Let me get used to being a father to just one for a while, shall we? I'm still trying to pick that up.'

'You're a great father.'

'Yes, but you have a head start on parenting—'

She took her hand off his face and gently smacked his shoulder. And he laughed, swaying her body a little deeper from side to side.

'That wasn't meant as a dig. I was just trying to say that you need to let me catch up some before you go shopping for a football team.'

'You can be horrible when you want to, you know.'

'I know. But you know that about me, just like I know that sometimes you can be stubborn and unreasonable. We learnt a lot of this stuff the first time round.'

'Yes, we did.'

'And that has to count in with the things to build on, doesn't it? Knowing those things and still wanting to be together means something.'

'Yes, it does.'

Rhiannon thought about the things he'd said at the table. 'You were counting friendship and working together in all this a minute ago too, weren't you?'

He squeezed her fingers. 'Yes, I thought you'd started to figure it out then, but you're obviously not as bright as I thought you were. If you were, then you'd have known that the *we're friends* line was complete nonsense—we were never *just friends*.'

For the first time since she'd met him all those years ago, she told him the absolute truth, without trying to hide anything.

'Well, what the hell else was I supposed to say? And maybe I was scared this time to hope you might want more, so I let myself assume that you were talking about the ingredients for working together as parents.'

'I was, but that wasn't the only reason.'

'And that was the part I was scared to look for.'

He smiled affectionately. 'Why?'

She smiled equally as affectionately, her gaze dropping to the top of his polo-neck—the same one he'd worn the first night she'd set eyes on him again. 'I think you did break my heart the first time you left me. I just refused to let myself believe I'd cared that much, so I made myself hate you instead. I was a kid back then. But I'm an adult now and I know exactly how I feel. If I got involved with you and you left again it would kill me. Or at least the part of me that might ever care that much again.' She glanced up at him from beneath long lashes. 'And then last night, when you suggested that ridiculous half a marriage—'

His arm tightened on her waist, holding her closer against his large frame, his words coming out on a rushed grumble. 'That didn't come across the way it was meant to. But, in fairness, you've had me on the run for a while and it took some time for me to get things straight in my head. I hadn't even thought about how I'd tell you.'

'And it's all straight in your head now?'

'Yes, crystal clear. I know what I want.' He leaned in for another long kiss. 'The only problem would have been what you wanted, especially after the mess I made last night—though it was the first real hint I'd got that you might actually feel something back. So I enrolled Lizzie's help to make a better attempt at it.'

'You two are always going to gang up on me, aren't you?' Not that it seemed like such a bad thing to her, considering where they were.

'Only for the good stuff.'

The music changed to a different beat in the background but Kane ignored it and kept the same slow swaying and circling as he took a breath and smiled a more confident smile. 'So by any chance did you miss me as much as I missed you this last while, even though we spend so much of our time arguing?'

'I missed you so much it hurt. Thanks. And we've always argued—we're both stubborn. All that was missing this time was the making up.'

He stopped swaying, removing his arm, releasing her fingers, so that he could frame her face with his hands and lean in to look into her eyes, as Lizzie had done when she'd examined his eyes and figured things out. 'I *really* want us to make up.'

Her palms flattened against the erratic beat of his heart, her smile broad. 'I love you, you idiot.'

A look of relief washed over his rugged features, removing any hint of the frowns he'd worn at the beginning from his face, so that he looked like a twenty-one-year-old again when he grinned at her. He let go of her face and crushed her to him, groaning by her ear as she hugged him back. 'Good!'

She laughed joyously against his chest, only just allowing herself to really believe that he cared as much as he did because he hadn't been sure of her feelings, had he? No matter what he said or did, what confidence he'd given the impression he had, until she'd said the words to his face, with her heart and soul in her eyes, he hadn't been completely sure.

They weren't so very different, not really. And maybe a subconscious part of her had recognized that matching need to let someone in coupled with an opposing defensive shield of anger and resentment to hold that very person away. Fear of letting go. They both had it, didn't they?

It was why, when he had let go with Lizzie, a part of Rhiannon's soul had known the man he was and had fallen in love with that man. Lizzie may have felt like the only thing holding them together, but she was simply the result of a bond that had already been there, if in a more fragile, youthful state.

'I love you too, Mac.' He whispered it huskily into her ear, pressing his lips into her hair before he rested his head against hers and held her tight.

She turned her head to tell him, 'Once you say that to me, you can't ever take it back. I won't ever let you go. You need to know that. So be sure, take some time if you need to.'

'I don't need time.' He stepped back a little to look down into her eyes, the familiar teasing light dancing in a blue clouded with a cornucopia of deep emotion, his baritone voice stronger, more confident. 'But if *you* want to take some time to get used to this, then that's okay, just so long as you know we'll need to discuss the *never in a million years* thing. I have a ring in my pocket that I can't give you for Valentine's Day next year if we can't negotiate the million years down to a more reasonable time frame.'

Her eyes widened in surprise again, even though she knew he'd probably surprise her on a daily basis for the rest of her life. 'You bought a ring?'

'I did, not that long ago, around about the time I figured out what it was I wanted. Didn't actually plan on it, but I saw it and it felt right buying it.' His sensuous mouth swung upwards into a smile. 'And I'd like the chance to prove my point about still having *this* when we're old and grey and round-shouldered. So, what do I have to do to change your mind about the time line?'

Her eyes shone. *'W-ell...'*

He stepped back and took her hand, dragging her towards the door. 'All right, if that's what it's going to take, I don't have a problem with that. We just need to tell our daughter she's having an early night.'

Rhiannon laughed loudly, neatly sidestepping him and then tugging him close, still laughing, so that they were pressed against the door. She drew his head down for the same heated kiss they had shared the night before and took it up a level, matching every slide of his lips, every stroke of his tongue, every small nip and intake of breath, while allowing her hands the freedom to roam up his arms, to hold on to his shoulders, to bury deep into the hair she'd always loved so much.

Until he mumbled against her mouth, 'Million years.'

She mumbled back, 'I might have lied about that.'

He lifted his head, shook it in disapproval. 'That was bad of you. Right, we'll spend time getting used to each other, then. Do this right this time. Though, just so you know, there's definitely marriage in our future.'

'I might need to see that ring.'

'No—you'll see it when I ask you to marry me.'

'I might not like the ring.' She batted her lashes at him. 'Go on—just a little look. Because I agree that there's definitely marriage in our future. And I happen to think it doesn't need to be all that far away. So I need to see the ring.'

He smiled, shaking his head as he looked at the upturned palm she was waving at his side. 'The ring comes with the question.'

Rhiannon let everything she felt for him shine in her eyes as she wiggled her fingers. 'Still want to see it. Weddings take ages to organize.'

Kane's beautiful blue eyes widened. 'Are you saying if I ask you now you'll say yes?'

'Why don't you ask me and see what happens?'

'Once this ring is on your finger, it stays on.'

'Yes, I know that.'

With a deep chuckle, joy lighting up his face, he reached into his pocket and produced the ring, holding it in front of her face for her to see, his brows lifting in question.

Rhiannon stared at it in wonder for a long silent moment, loving that he had chosen a stone the same colour as his eyes. 'It's beautiful.' She whispered the words. 'So ask me.'

'You're never going to do what I expect you to do, are you?'

'No, but you already knew that. Ask me.'

He twisted the ring back and forth between his thumb and forefinger, the light catching on the stone so it appeared almost hypnotic, especially when accompanied by a husky baritone voice filled with emotion.

'Marry me. Make us officially the family we already are. I love you; I probably always have. And life's too short to waste time; I know that better than most.'

She grinned like an idiot, her eyes filling with tears at the same time. How could she not want to live a lifetime with this man?

'I love you. So it's yes—a *million* times yes.'

Kane leaned in and kissed her again, for a very long time, taking a moment to smile down at her heavy eyes and swollen lips before she informed him with a sigh, 'You do know you've just ruined your chances of ever topping this Valentine's Day ever again?'

He reached for her hand, grinning wickedly as he slipped the ring into place. 'I think you'll find that I'm capable of more than a card and a box of chocolates every other year or so. You wait and see.'

Rhiannon pulled him close again, knowing that at some point they really should go and tell Lizzie that her romantic meal had done the trick. But when they bumped back against the door a voice yelled from the hallway, 'Are you two kissing?'

His mouth hovering over hers, Kane's gaze rose to fix on the door. 'Yes, we are! So shoo!'

A loud celebration commenced beyond the door, gradually dimming as Lizzie went further up the hall.

They laughed together before his mouth lowered to hers again.

'And we're going to be kissing for a long, long while to make up for lost time. We've ten years' worth of making up to do. Happy Valentine's Day.'

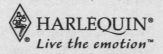

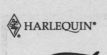

HARLEQUIN®

Mediterranean NIGHTS™

*Things are heating up
aboard Alexandra's Dream....*

Coming in March 2008

ISLAND HEAT

by

Sarah Mayberry

It's been eight years since Tory Sanderson found
out that Ben Cooper seduced her to win a bet...
and eight years since she got her revenge. Now
aboard *Alexandra's Dream* as a guest lecturer for
her cookbook, she is shocked to discover the
guest chef joining her is none other than Ben!
And when these two ex-lovers reunite, the heat
starts to climb...in and out of the kitchen!

*Available in March 2008
wherever books are sold.*

www.eHarlequin.com

HM38969

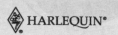

REQUEST YOUR FREE BOOKS!
2 FREE NOVELS PLUS 2
FREE GIFTS!

HARLEQUIN ROMANCE®

From the Heart, For the Heart

YES! Please send me 2 FREE Harlequin Romance® novels and my 2 FREE gifts. After receiving them, if I don't wish to receive any more books, I can return the shipping statement marked "cancel." If I don't cancel, I will receive 4 brand-new novels every month and be billed just $3.57 per book in the U.S., or $4.05 per book in Canada, plus 25¢ shipping and handling per book and applicable taxes, if any*. That's a savings of over 15% off the cover price! I understand that accepting the 2 free books and gifts places me under no obligation to buy anything. I can always return a shipment and cancel at any time. Even if I never buy another book from Harlequin, the two free books and gifts are mine to keep forever.

114 HDN EEV7 314 HDN EEWK

Name	(PLEASE PRINT)	
Address		Apt.
City	State/Prov.	Zip/Postal Code

Signature (if under 18, a parent or guardian must sign)

Mail to the **Harlequin Reader Service®**:
IN U.S.A.: P.O. Box 1867, Buffalo, NY 14240-1867
IN CANADA: P.O. Box 609, Fort Erie, Ontario L2A 5X3

Not valid to current Harlequin Romance subscribers.

Want to try two free books from another line?
Call 1-800-873-8635 or visit www.morefreebooks.com.

* Terms and prices subject to change without notice. NY residents add applicable sales tax. Canadian residents will be charged applicable provincial taxes and GST. This offer is limited to one order per household. All orders subject to approval. Credit or debit balances in a customer's account(s) may be offset by any other outstanding balance owed by or to the customer. Please allow 4 to 6 weeks for delivery.

Your Privacy: Harlequin is committed to protecting your privacy. Our Privacy Policy is available online at www.eHarlequin.com or upon request from the Reader Service. From time to time we make our lists of customers available to reputable firms who may have a product or service of interest to you. If you would prefer we not share your name and address, please check here. ☐

HR07

Inside ROMANCE

Stay up-to-date on all your romance reading news!

Inside Romance is a FREE quarterly newsletter highlighting our upcoming series releases and promotions.

Visit
www.eHarlequin.com/InsideRomance
to sign up to receive our complimentary newsletter today!